The Scream

BILL MYERS

Tyndale House Publishers, Inc. Wheaton, Illinois

For George Lord,
a friend in good times
and bad

If you need wisdom—if you want to know what
God wants you to do—ask him, and he will gladly
tell you.

James 1:5

Designed by Beth Sparkman

Edited by Karen Ball

Published in association with the literary agency of Alive
Communications, Inc., 1465 Kelly Johnson Blvd., Suite 320,
Colorado Springs, CO 80920.

Scripture quotations are taken from the *Holy Bible,* New
Living Translation, copyright © 1996. Used by permission of
Tyndale House Publishers, Inc., Wheaton, Illinois 60189. All
rights reserved.

ISBN 0-8423-5970-2

Printed in the United States of America

03 02 01 00 99 98
7   6   5   4   3   2   1

1

At the Poseidon Arena in San Francisco, the megapopular heavy-metal rock band The Scream tore through their last set in front of a packed house. The music was loud and the show was exciting—a combination of the latest high-tech special effects and bizarre makeup and costumes.

Scream lead singer Tommy Doland had a red pentagram painted across his face so that his intense dark eyes peered out from the center. His long hair was coal black except for a great shock in the front that was dyed bright blue. His outfit was part Roman emperor and part Darth Vadar as his long cape billowed out behind while he strutted the length of the stage singing:

> "I'm riding on wings of fire.
> I'm burning the fields of desire.
> In touch with the overlord,
> He takes me higher. . . ."

On the word *higher* his voice catapulted into a loud shriek, one of the band's trademarks, and the audience's response was immediate and frenzied. The audience itself was something to behold. Dressed in homemade versions of the same costumes and makeup as the band members, the crowd seemed even angrier than the band. They moved constantly, slamming into each other with a fierceness that was somewhere between a wild, uncontrolled dance and an outright riot.

Drummer Mike Parsek looked toward the angry wave of humanity as he hammered out the driving beat and wondered just how close the crowd was to losing control. Three kids had been hospitalized last week at their concert in Denver, and Mike was the first to admit that it could've been a lot worse. Kids had been crushed to death in rock concerts—not theirs, but it happened. Even so, building frenzy was the key element to the band's show. After all, the kids came because they *wanted* that kind of excitement, a wild ride.

Mike scanned the screaming fans again and frowned. Sometimes he worried how that ride might end.

Singer Tommy Doland never worried about that part of the concert. His method of operation was always the same: Take it higher, drive it harder, push it farther.

A highlight of the show was always Mike's drum solo, and no matter how much Mike pushed it, Doland always wanted it to go a little farther. For this tour the drum solo had become a big production number loaded with special effects. The climax of the solo now included the eruption of a giant fire cannon that had been made to look like a fierce dragon. When Mike's solo reached its peak, the two huge flamethrowers concealed in the dragon's mechanical throat blasted out twenty-foot streaks of fire directly over the heads of those in the audience, making them scream in delight.

It was time for Mike's solo, and he jumped in with a vengeance. As he increased the volume and tempo, he felt the tension build—in the audience, who expected something spectacular at this point, and in himself, as he got ready for the coming explosion and burst of flame.

Launching into the final pattern, Mike eyed stage manager Billy Phelps, whose job it was to ignite the fire cannon. As usual, Billy was nodding along with the beat, one finger on the button, ready to fire. Mike steeled himself for the blast and nodded slightly, but the visual cue was unnecessary. Phelps knew the timing by heart, and he pressed the button.

There was a brief hesitation and then a crackling sound that Mike had never heard before. A puff of smoke came from the dragon's mouth. This was followed by a clinking sound that came off like a groan from the pit of the dragon's stomach—and then silence.

Something was wrong.

Mike breathed a sigh of relief. Part of him was glad it hadn't worked. Every time the cannon went off, he wondered if the kids in the first row were going to become burnt offerings. Then, out of the corner of his eye,

Mike caught a glimpse of Tommy Doland. The lead singer appeared to be laughing.

Later on in the show, the band wailed away as Doland sang their latest hit, "Army of the Night." Meanwhile, Billy Phelps worked on the broken dragon.

"I can't figure out why this thing isn't firing," he muttered to himself as he examined the circuitry of the control panel for the fire cannon. "Everything here looks OK. Must be up in the barrel. Better cut the power."

With that, he switched off the control board and began crawling underneath the cannon. Onstage Doland sang:

> "Army of the night,
> Not afraid to fight,
> Marching into danger
> Without any light."

As Doland twisted and writhed across the stage, the crowd screamed, and guitarist Jackie Vee ripped into a searing solo. Meanwhile, Billy Phelps had worked his way to the end of the cannon's barrel.

Doland continued singing:

"Army of the night,
The master's wishes soar,
Risking our life
To fight his holy war."

At these words, as though an unseen hand moved it, the power switch on the fire cannon's control panel vibrated to the "On" position. Unaware of this, Billy Phelps reached inside the barrel to shine his flashlight down the dragon's mouth. Meanwhile, Doland continued to sing:

"Army of the night,
Unholy alliance,
Our soul submitted
For your compliance."

Suddenly, the loading mechanism of the fire cannon began to shake, but since Billy was at the opposite end, he didn't notice.

Mike Parsek looked up from the drums, sensing a difference in the cannon's vibration. He looked over to the control panel and saw that it had switched to "On." Then, with horror, he saw the small red light on the loading mechanism also flicker on.

The cannon was about to fire!

Mike looked to Billy, but the stage manager was leaning down so far into the cannon that only his legs could be seen.

"Billy!" Mike shouted. "Get out of there!"

Phelps didn't hear him. The loading mechanism vibrated, and the light on the panel shifted from red to green.

Mike knew he'd never reach Billy in time, so he hurled one of his drumsticks at the stage manager's legs. It connected, and a bewildered Phelps pulled his head out from the cannon to see what was happening. Spotting the stick on the floor, he looked over to Mike, who waved frantically for him to get out of the way.

But there was no time. The cannon fired.

The flame that shot from the dragon's head was a wall of fire. It shot over Phelps and out across the stage. Grant Simone, the band's bass player, turned just in time to see his amplifier catch fire. With a yelp, he dove out of the way.

Phelps was not so lucky. His clothes were aflame.

The crowd screamed, unsure if this was part of the show or an accident. Mike leaped off his drum riser and ran toward Billy. As he passed Doland, he snatched the lead singer's cape and charged for the burning man. Leaping through the air, Mike landed on top of Phelps and knocked him to the

7

ground. Quickly he began to smother the fire with the cape.

After several long, terrifying seconds, it was over.

Fifteen minutes later Billy Phelps was being carried off in an ambulance and the police were clearing the auditorium.

Onstage the road crew began to break down the elaborate set. Mike, still stunned, stood by his drums watching one of the road-ies begin to dismantle the huge fire cannon.

"Hey, Mike," the roadie said, "why didn't Billy shut that thing down while he worked on it? Doesn't he know better than that?"

Mike looked at the roadie for a long moment. "He did shut it down. I saw him do it. The thing . . . it kicked on by itself."

The roadie looked at Mike as if he were nuts, but he didn't say anything.

Mike left the stage and headed for Doland's dressing room. He knocked twice on the door.

"Come in," Doland said.

Mike opened the door to see Doland standing before the mirror, still wearing his stage makeup. "Oh, it's the hero of the hour. Come on in, Mike. What's up?"

"Doland . . . I know for a fact that Billy shut that cannon down before he started working on it. I saw him do it. The thing came on by itself like some sort of . . ." He trailed off, not sure what to say.

Doland smiled strangely. "Some sort of what, Mike?"

"Some sort of . . . monster. Like it had a mind of its own."

Doland laughed gruffly. "Come now, Mikey. A well-churched boy like you doesn't buy into that sort of nonsense, does he? Sounds like black magic, and you don't believe in black magic now, do you?"

Doland's expression was taunting.

Mike turned away. "I've told you before. I don't like you teasing me about my father."

Doland gave a look of mock sympathy. "Oh, you mean the good reverend? I wouldn't dream of it, Mike."

"How can you be joking around like this with Billy in the hospital?"

Doland shrugged. "Billy's going to be all right. You heard the medic. He'll be OK, thanks to that quick business you did with my cape—which, by the way, you owe me for."

Mike couldn't believe his ears. "You're worried about the cost of the cape?"

Doland shook his head. "Not really. I know that what happened here tonight is good for business. This little accident will sell a hundred thousand more albums for us by the end of the week."

Mike shook his head. "It's not about money, Doland. It's like I've been saying: Things are out of hand. This devil stuff has gone too far."

Doland squinted his eyes and mimicked Mike's voice. *"This devil stuff?* Little church boy afraid of the big bad devil stuff, eh? Sometimes I think you're in the wrong band, Mikey boy."

Mike knew he was on risky ground since Doland could easily get him kicked out of the band if he wanted to push the issue, but still he continued. "Listen to me for a minute, Doland. Something has changed. Can't you see that?"

"I see far more than you, Mikey. But don't sweat it. I know what I'm doing."

Mike shook his head. This was getting him nowhere. He started to leave, then paused at the door. "It used to be fun, Tommy, but . . . don't you see? We're losing control—"

Doland cut him off with a nasty laugh. "I haven't lost control of anything, Mikey. Everything is just the way I want it."

It had not been one of Scott's better days. . . .

First the church's junior high camping trip was canceled because they couldn't find enough chaperons.

Then Mom asked him to clean his room. Naturally, he figured that meant piling everything that was on the floor up onto his bed so he could go play baseball with the guys. That part was fine. It was coming home and finding Mom steamed that wasn't so fine. That and the discipline she had in mind for him.

"I still don't see why I have to wash these stupid windows," he complained for the tenth time.

"Because they're dirty," Mom replied.

"But windows aren't my job. They should be Becka's. Cleaning is for girls."

Mom sighed. They'd had this conversation in one form or another several hundred times. "Cleaning is everyone's work, Scott. And if you'd cleaned your room the way I asked you to, I wouldn't have given you this extra duty."

"You said you wanted to see the floor of my room. Well?"

Mom shook her head. "I also wanted to see your bed. You're too old to pull a stunt like that."

"Obviously I'm not," Scott mumbled as he went back to wiping the living-room window. Outside he could see his older sister, Rebecca. She was playing football with her sort-of boyfriend, Ryan. Scott waited until

Ryan lobbed her a pass before rapping on the window to distract her. "Hey, Becka!" With any luck she'd turn to him just in time to get whacked on the head.

But Rebecca wasn't falling for it. She carefully caught the ball before turning toward her brother in the house. "Yes, Scott?" she called pleasantly. "May I help you?"

Scott grimaced, then called out, "Why don't you guys come in here and give me a hand with these windows!"

Rebecca laughed. "No way. You earned that job."

Scott went back to his mumbling. "Might as well clean windows. With the camping trip canceled, it's going to be another boring week. I *never* get to do *anything.*"

"What are you harping about now?" Mom asked as she walked through the room.

"Nothing," Scott answered. "I was just wondering why we never get to do anything fun."

Mom looked aghast. "How can you say that? You've been traveling all over the place. You got to visit Louisiana; your sister went to Europe."

"That's different," Scott whined. "We were helping Z."

Z was their friend from the Internet. Although they'd never met him in person, he'd led them into all sorts of intense adventures helping various people.

"Are you telling me that you never have any fun on these trips?" Mom asked.

Scott shrugged. "A little, I suppose. But Z always sends us to goofy places. Why can't he send us someplace exciting to do something fun?"

"Let me guess. . . ." Mom pretended to search for an answer. "Because Z isn't your personal cruise director?"

Scott frowned. But only for a second because outside he saw a large FedEx truck stopping directly in front of their house. He raced past Mom and headed outside, even managing to beat his sister to the truck. The driver laughed and handed him a large envelope. "Sign here, son."

Scott signed the form and quickly opened the envelope.

"What is it?" Rebecca asked.

Scott examined the contents. "I'm not sure . . . some airline tickets, a hotel reservation, and some other kind of tickets. . . . *Wow!*"

By now Mom was out the door as well. "Wow, what?"

Scott was so excited he could hardly speak. "It's the concert tickets from Z. . . . Our trip to L.A. It's been like a month since

he mentioned it. He sent us three free tickets *and* backstage passes to see The Scream
in their Los Angeles appearance."

"The who?" Mom asked.

"The Scream," he explained. "They're the
hottest band in the country . . . and we're
going to get to meet them!"

Becka and Ryan looked at each other in
surprise. Tickets to a Scream concert?

Mom took the package and read the note.
"There's a ticket for me, too," she said. "I
suppose I could use a short vacation."

Scott was all smiles. "Then we can go?"

"Well . . . I . . ."

"Great. Just wait'll the guys hear about
this!" He turned to his sister. "Is this cool or
what?"

Rebecca looked at him before finally managing a lame, "Yeah . . . cool."

But the feeling in her gut told her she was
anything but thrilled about this. The Scream
was popular with all the kids at school, but
from what she'd heard of their stuff, it was
definitely heavy metal—and definitely flirt-
ing with dark, satanic stuff. Stuff that always
gave her the creeps. Even now she felt a cool
shiver crawl across her skin.

What possible reason could Z have for
wanting them to meet The Scream?

2

Scott lost no time telling all his friends about his good fortune. Already there had been at least four kids at the door, each holding Scream albums and photos and asking if he could get them autographed for them. Of course, Scott said it would be no problem. In fact, it seemed to Rebecca that with each new person he talked to, he made a bigger deal out of this trip. Before long he'd gone from a member of the audience to "a personal friend of the band."

"I never said that," Scott argued after Becka brought it up.

"Sure you did. Something like that."

"I never said I was a personal friend of the band. Darryl asked me how I got the tickets, and I said 'a close personal friend.' *He* said, 'You're friends with the band?' I just didn't say otherwise."

"You nodded as you closed the door," Rebecca argued. "And you *know* Darryl is out telling everyone that you're pals with The Scream."

Scott's face lit up with a sly smile. "You think so? Cool."

"It's not exactly telling the truth, Scotty."

Scott shrugged. "And it's not exactly lying."

"Mom might have other ideas . . . and I know Dad would." Bringing up their deceased father was a low blow, and Becka regretted it as soon as she'd said it—and as soon as she saw the look on Scotty's face. She touched his arm. "I'm sorry. I don't know what Dad would say. Forget it. I don't care what your friends think anyway."

Scott nodded. That was obviously fine with him.

"But—" Becka changed the subject—"I think we should at least E-mail Z. I think we should find out why it's so important to him that we see The Scream."

"Why?" Scott asked as Mom entered the room with laundry.

"We need more information," Rebecca answered. "Right now all we know is that we're supposed to meet their drummer."

"All you knew in Transylvania was that you were supposed to meet Jaimie," Scott replied. "The rest just happens . . . kinda like falling off a log."

"I hope what happened in Transylvania is not your idea of falling off a log." Rebecca scowled. With that she got up and headed into the kitchen.

A moment later Mom followed her. "What's the matter, honey?" Mom asked. "You don't want to go to L.A.?"

"It's not really that," Becka answered. "It's just . . . The Scream. . . . I mean, they're great and all, but they're really into the black-magic stuff—skulls and devils all the way. I know most of it's just an act . . . but it's not really an act I want to see."

Mom nodded. "I'm surprised Z wants you associating with them, much less listening to their music."

"Me too," Rebecca agreed.

"Unless . . ."

"Unless what?"

"Unless Z figures that by going you'll be helping them someway."

Rebecca knew Mom was right. That's how it had always been with Z. He never sent them someplace unless it was to help. And Becka knew something else, too. She knew it wasn't about whether or not she liked the music. It was about whether or not she wanted to help the people making that music.

And the truth was, part of her didn't. As far as she could tell, they were dark, satanic, and just plain nasty. Maybe they were nice guys under all that goop and three-foot hair, but they were definitely not her idea of good company.

And yet, if they needed help . . .

"I guess we should probably pray about it," Rebecca sighed.

Mom nodded. There was no missing the pride welling up in her eyes. She knew this was one of the reasons Z had selected her children. Becka was cautious . . . but when it came to making decisions, she always let God have his way.

~

Mike Parsek sat in the back of the limo as it came to a halt. It was one of three stretch limos that pulled up in front of the Beverly Wilshire Hotel. Mike sighed. He was in no hurry to get out as he watched The Scream's entourage pour out of the cars. The other three members of the band got out of the first limo. Out of the second came two publicists, one road manager, a sound engineer, a light guy, and four roadies. Mike shared the third limo with clothes and guitars.

He was the last to enter the hotel lobby, where the scene was taking on epic proportions. It never ceased to amaze him. Wherever the band went, they were like modern-day kings. Wherever one of the band members turned there was someone to wait on him. Then, of course, there were the fans—screaming, shouting, and begging for autographs.

Mike and the others signed a few autographs and exchanged small talk with a segment of their adoring legion. Then Doland nodded slightly to the three burly security men waiting nearby. Instantly the hulks moved into action and smoothly separated the crowd from the band.

The security guys were pros. Their sheer massiveness eased the crowd away as they escorted the band to the elevator. Mike gave a sigh of relief. By now the road manager had secured their rooms, and the publicists

and tech guys scrambled for what accommo-
dations were left. The roadies would go on
to the auditorium and set up for most of the
night. Then they'd sleep in the van.

Twenty minutes later, Mike and the other
band members were in one of their rooms
eating steak sandwiches and drinking exotic-
looking bottles of a beer made in the Afri-
can country of Chad. It was bottled
especially for them by a guy in Trenton, New
Jersey, whom they paid a thousand dollars a
week for the service. Actually, *they* didn't pay
it. Their record label did—just like it paid
for a hundred other little extras that came
under the heading of "touring expenses."
Mike couldn't help but smile. Yes, sir, they
didn't call it rock 'n' roll because it was a
conservative business.

"I think we should start with 'Army of the
Night' tomorrow," Tommy Doland was saying between sips of beer. "It's what they want
to hear."

Jackie Vee polished his guitar. It was a
1956 Gibson Les Paul—worth about ten
grand—and it seldom left his side. "We can
if you want." He shrugged. "Only don't we
usually save it for a grand finale at the end
of the night?"

Doland swigged his beer. "I just want to
get it over with. Get all the blasted shouting

over with up front so we can enjoy the rest
of the gig."

Mike knew that it was best for him to stay
out of Doland's way during such discussions,
but he couldn't resist. "You don't want them
to cheer?"

"Of course I want them to cheer," Doland
sneered. "I want them to pass out from
cheering their heads off. But I don't want
them calling out for 'Army of the Night' all
night long and not paying attention to our
other songs. Especially the new ones. The
ones *not* on the album."

Mike nodded. "But that new stuff, you
know it hasn't been going over with the audience like some of our older—"

"That's 'cause they don't listen," Doland
interrupted. There was no missing the edge
to his voice. "We've got to help them get
into these new songs."

"Some say the new songs are way too
dark," Mike said so softly that he almost
wasn't heard.

But Doland heard. "They're too dark
because the idiots don't understand what
we're trying to say!" Doland snapped. He
stopped; then the sarcastic smile crossed his
face again. "Like some of you," he went on,
his mocking eyes riveted on Mike, "they just
don't *get* it." With that, he patted Mike on

the head, got up, and walked out the door, heading to his room.

Mike watched him go and then looked at Grant Simone, who was sanding the frets on his bass guitar with a worn piece of sandpaper. "See what I mean?" Mike said. "That's how he is all the time now."

Grant shrugged and went on sanding the frets. "I'm thinking about redoing these frets again."

Mike shook his head. "If you'd stop sanding them all the time, they'd last longer. Listen, don't you guys think Doland is acting weird?"

"So what?" Jackie Vee argued. "So the pressure is getting to him a little. I didn't hear you asking to be left out of the limo, Mikey."

Grant nodded. "Or these fancy rooms or the fame or the chicks—"

"Or all that beautiful, cold hard cash." Jackie Vee grinned.

Mike looked at them both, wanting to respond, to tell them they were wrong . . . but he couldn't. They were right.

He looked away and let out a sad, lonely sigh.

~

Rebecca was still pretty unsure about the trip. Even on Sunday morning as she packed. The whole family had come to look forward to these "little getaways." Usually all three of them went. The travel kind of reminded Rebecca of their missionary days down in South America. But this time something was bugging her. It was way down deep in her stomach, and she couldn't seem to ignore it. She'd tried contacting Z earlier on the Internet, but he wasn't logged on. Nor had he left any E-mail. For the time being at least, it looked like they were on their own.

"Hurry up, Rebecca, it's almost nine-thirty," Mom called from the kitchen. It was nearly time to leave for church, and Rebecca had been dawdling, thinking about what it would be like to be in L.A. with Mom, her goofy brother, and four guys who wore capes, painted symbols on their faces, and had hair longer than hers.

"Hey, Beck, where's my Levi's jacket?" Scott called from his room.

"You don't have a Levi's jacket," Rebecca answered. "It's mine."

"Well, where's *your* Levi's jacket, then?"

"In *my* closet, where it belongs . . . and no, you can't borrow it again."

"Why not?"

Rebecca sighed. "Because last time you left it outside in the sun with a candy bar in the pocket . . . remember?"

"Oh yeah. C'mon, I promise I won't do that. It's too early for candy, and Mom doesn't let me eat it in church anyway."

Sometimes Rebecca couldn't believe her brother. "That's not the point. Remember, I told you that you couldn't wear it again if you didn't take care of it."

"I took care of it. I just forgot about the candy bar, that's all."

"You also left it wadded up on the floor."

"So?" Scott clearly did not have a clue what the problem was here.

"So, you were supposed to hang it up."

"I leave *all* my clothes on the floor."

"I'll vouch for that," Mom said, joining in. "You guys better hurry and get dressed. We have to go if we're going to make church and still catch that plane."

Scott tapped on Rebecca's door. "Beck . . . c'mon. I need that jacket."

Rebecca combed her hair in front of the dresser mirror. "No."

Scott was persistent. "Can I come in?

With another sigh, she opened the door. "Why? You can't borrow my jacket. And *where* did you get that shirt? Mom's not going to let you wear that to church."

It was the official Scream T-shirt. Four hairy guys scowling and holding skulls in their hands. "It's Darryl's," Scott answered.

"And I'm not wearing it to church. Just let me borrow the jacket. You can borrow something of mine."

Becka closed her eyes for a moment. It just wasn't worth the fight. With a shake of her head, she opened up her closet and pulled out the jeans jacket. "Here. Just be nice to me on the plane."

"Sure," Scott said, grabbing the jacket from her. "I always am."

Once again Rebecca felt that woozy sensation deep in her stomach. She'd been feeling it every time she thought about going to L.A. And now here it was the very day they were leaving and she was feeling worse than ever. Earlier, they'd all prayed and felt it was something God wanted them to do. But still . . .

What are we doing this for, Lord? she asked. *You can't possibly want us to be around these guys, can you?*

She waited, but no answer came.

A half hour later they were in church. The service helped a little. The choir did one of Rebecca's favorite songs, and the drama team put on a funny skit. Finally she was starting to relax . . . until the pastor began his sermon. And then she got tense all over again.

"I want to ask you this morning, why do

you suppose that Jesus dined with tax collectors and prostitutes?" he began. "Do you think there was better food in that part of town?"

Several people chuckled, and the pastor continued, "Do you think he enjoyed the company of those people more than he did the company of priests and scribes? Well, maybe he did. The tax collectors and prostitutes were probably more down to earth and a lot more real. We know Jesus was not a big fan of hypocrisy, and the Pharisees were loaded with it. But I think the real reason Jesus dined with what was considered a bunch of lowlifes was that he wanted to reach them. To communicate with them. He didn't come just for the priests and scribes. He came for *all* people. How could he expect these people to accept what he was saying if he didn't accept them? They were sinners, to be sure. But aren't we all? Fortunately, Jesus sees beyond that. He sees all of us—social outcasts or not—as people. And he loves us all."

Becka's stomach was churning like a cement mixer, but her mind was focused on the words. She was hearing something from God. She knew it.

"Yes, Jesus is also the great Judge, but he didn't come to judge—not then. He came to

love those who were trapped in darkness.
And love begins with acceptance . . . not of
the sin, but of the sinner. As those who seek
to follow Christ, can we do any less? We're
called not only to accept those who are different from us but, like Paul did on his jour-
neys, to go the extra mile to bond with
them. We need to understand them so we
can speak to their hearts. For Jesus, it was
the prostitutes and the tax collectors. Who is
it for us? Who are the lost *we* are to reach?"

Rebecca slowly nodded. *OK, Lord, I get it.*
And she did. She was going to L.A. She was
going to meet the band. She would talk with
them, hang out with them . . . even accept
them. And when the time came, she would
have the courage to speak God's truth to
them.

At least, she hoped she would.

3

The main Los
Angeles airport was LAX. That's what the
people called it. No long fancy name after
some former city politician. No warm-fuzzy
sounding name with *hills* or *briar* or *crest* in
it. Just the basic deal.

It was very L.A.

From the plane, Rebecca and Scott could

see mountains, but they'd seen mountains before—bigger ones than these—back in South America. They could also see the ocean, but they'd seen that before too. It really wasn't until they were on the ground in the airport that they began to see the real sights of L.A.

"Hey, isn't that Suzanne Winters?" Scott piped up as soon as they reached the baggage-claim area. "You know—the star of that big television show. Right over there."

"Scott, don't point," Rebecca whispered in embarrassment. "People don't like that."

"How would you know?" he retorted. "How many stars have you seen?"

"C'mon, kids, we've got to get our bags," Mom called.

Out in the parking lot, they caught a shuttle to their hotel. "Why do they call it a shuttle?" Scott wanted to know. "It's a bus."

"They call it a shuttle because it goes back and forth between the hotel and the airport," Rebecca explained.

"Yeah, I know," Scott replied. "A bus."

Becka blew the hair out of her eyes and heaved her suitcase up into the luggage area. As they headed up the freeway on-ramp, they could see heavy smoke off in the distance.

"What's that?" Rebecca asked. "Looks like a big fire."

The man sitting across from them answered, "There's a brushfire burning out of control in the mountains. It's headed toward Malibu."

"Wow!" Scott replied, in awe of the great pillars of smoke.

Rebecca's stomach was still acting up. She winced slightly and shifted in her seat.

Mom turned to her. "What's the matter, honey?"

"Oh, it's just my stomach. That sure looks like a huge fire."

"No biggie," Scott said, suddenly sounding very authoritative. "There's some kind of natural disaster going on almost every day in Los Angeles. My teacher said the place is like a natural-disaster theme park."

Somehow that didn't help Becka's stomach.

Eventually the shuttle cruised into Beverly Hills.

"Cool!" Scott exclaimed, his face glued to the window. "This is where a lot of the movie stars live. Check out the size of that house."

"And look at those shops," Rebecca added, pointing in a different direction. "Could we do some shopping while we're here, Mom?"

Mom nodded. "A little. But not at those places, honey. That's Rodeo Drive."

She pronounced it *Ro-day-o* Drive, but Scott hadn't heard. He also read the sign. "It says Rodeo Drive," he mused, looking at it. "You don't want to shop there, Beck. Probably all cowboy clothes and stuff like that."

"Scotty," Rebecca snickered, "Rodeo Drive is known for having some of the finest fashion stores in all the world."

"And they're *very* expensive," Mom added.

"That's *so* L.A.," Scott quipped. "Expect you to pay a fortune for cowboy clothes."

Before Becka could respond, the shuttle pulled into the hotel parking lot. All three family members sat in stunned silence. The place was beautiful. Bellhops were everywhere, loading baggage onto little golden carts. Rich people in rich clothes strolled back and forth. And just outside Scott's window was the longest car he'd ever seen.

"Look at that!" he exclaimed. "It's like a double limo!"

"They call that a stretch," the man across the aisle said.

"No wonder," Scott replied. "Must be a stretch to afford it."

They watched as a long-haired man with dark sunglasses and a shock of bright blue hair climbed out of the stretch limo and started walking toward the hotel. But just before he headed up the steps, he stopped suddenly. He slowly turned around to stare hard at the shuttle bus.

"Hey, isn't that Tommy Doland?" Scott asked as they rose to their feet and headed for the door of the bus.

Becka nodded. "Why do you suppose he's looking at us?" she asked, feeling her stomach tighten again.

No one had an answer.

Doland stood there, watching the people get off the shuttle. Rebecca was the first to reach the exit, and as she stepped down the stairs, she glanced up to see the singer still staring. He had taken off his dark sunglasses and looked like he was trying to glare a hole right through her.

She felt a cold shiver run through her body.

Then, just as abruptly as he'd stopped, Tommy Doland snapped his sunglasses back on and hurried up the steps to the hotel.

It took a moment for Rebecca to start breathing again.

"He was looking right at you!" Scott exclaimed in excitement.

She nodded, numb.

"You should have said something! At least waved. I bet he could have taken us right to Mike Parsek."

"Those are not our instructions," Rebecca said, finally finding her voice. "We're supposed to see him after the show. Besides . . ."

"Besides what?" Scotty pressed as they headed toward the hotel.

Rebecca looked at her brother and frowned. What she'd felt . . . it had been the same sensation that she'd experienced back when they were battling a so-called guardian angel that had decided to take up residence in Becka's friend Julie. She swallowed and finally answered, "When he was staring at me, it was like I couldn't speak. Like I was choking—" She met her brother's eyes. "Scotty, I couldn't breathe."

⚡

Mike detected the faint smell of marijuana smoke the moment he knocked on Jackie Vee's hotel-room door. There was no answer, so he knocked again. Then the door opened slowly, and Jackie peered out at him.

"Hey, Jackie. Got a minute?"

"Sure. C'mon in."

As soon as Mike closed the door, Jackie took out a small silver case, about the size of a pack of cigarettes. He opened it and took out a joint. From the looks of him, it wasn't his first. "Want to get high, man?"

Mike shook his head. "No, it throws off my

timing. We've got to rehearse in a couple of hours. I hope tonight's show goes well. I want us to feel really good going into that upcoming cable broadcast. Forty million viewers, man."

"Should be good." Jackie nodded. "Will Billy be back for that?"

"Should be. I talked to him a while ago. Sounds like he's doing pretty well. You should call him."

Jackie took a long hit off the joint and stared blankly into space.

"I said you should call him," Mike repeated.

Jackie looked up, squinting like he was trying to focus. "What? . . . Oh yeah." He waved his hand dismissively. "I'm too tired to call him now. Maybe after rehearsal."

Mike nodded, but he knew Jackie would never remember to call. He probably wouldn't even remember they'd talked. "Listen," he asked, "what are we going to do about Doland? I can hardly talk to him anymore."

"He's off on his own trip, that's for sure," Jackie agreed. "But he gets the crowd going, doesn't he? He plays the audience like I play this guitar."

Mike nodded but pressed the issue. "I talked to him about Billy getting hurt. It was like he didn't even care. He just said it would sell more albums."

Jackie took another hit. "Probably will. Doland knows that stuff."

"Yeah," Mike agreed. "But does he care about anybody?"

Jackie didn't seem to hear. He was just sucking on the joint and staring at nothing. Mike knew from past experience that the conversation was over. Jackie was too high to listen to anything that required thought. He stood up. "I've got to go. See you at rehearsal."

He was out the door and starting down the hall before Jackie managed to call after him, "OK . . . see you, Mike."

He headed for the elevator and pushed the button. A moment later, the door opened to reveal Tommy Doland.

"Doland . . . I . . ." For some reason, Doland's appearance startled him. Mike found himself feeling guilty, like he'd been "caught" at being disloyal.

Tommy smiled, but there was something very unpleasant in the way his lips curled. "Hi ya, Mikey. Your room here? No, that's right. Your room is on the sixth floor. Jackie's room is here . . . just down the hall, right?"

"Right." Mike tried to smile. "We were

just—" He broke off. Doland's smile had turned to ice.

"I know what you were doing, Mikey. You were trying to turn Jackie against me."

Mike stared at him, stunned—and very uneasy at the look in Tommy's eyes. "No, I wasn't . . . not really. I'm just worried."

"You should be worried, Mikey. You cross me again and I'll fry you."

Mike was shocked by the threat. "What? *Fry* me? What is *that* supposed to—"

Doland cut him off. "Fry you? My, my, getting a bit paranoid, aren't we?" He smiled again, his eyes glazing over. "I said I'd *fire* you, Mikey . . . from the band." The smile broadened. "You just need to be more careful now, don't you? When you listen to people, I mean." Doland stood there in the elevator, glaring at Mike as the steel door closed, leaving Mike staring blankly at it.

"This place is unbelievable," Scott muttered as he studied his reflection in the mirrored walls of the elevator. Rebecca shook her head. It didn't take much to entertain some people.

Just then there was a loud ding. The elevator door opened, and she moved to step out. "Our floor, Scott—" but she broke off and stared in surprise. There, right in front of her, was Mike Parsek. In fact, if she hadn't known better, Rebecca could have sworn he'd been staring at the elevator, waiting for them.

Scott recognized him immediately. "Uh . . ." But for the first time in his life he seemed to be speechless.

Rebecca grabbed his arm and pulled him from the elevator as Mike moved past them to enter it. At last Scotty found his voice . . . well, at least some of it. "Hey . . . hi . . . uh . . ."

But as Mike turned and the elevator doors closed, he was not looking at Scott. His gaze was locked on Rebecca. And he seemed very impressed.

The two stood in stunned silence. Finally Scott spoke. "Wow . . . did you see him check you out?"

Rebecca was dumbfounded. Most of the boys back at school didn't even know she existed. But clearly this guy did. And he just happened to be a rock star!

"That was Mike Parsek!" Scott exclaimed. "The one we're supposed to talk to! Why didn't you say something?"

Rebecca tried to swallow, but her mouth was as dry as cotton. "Why didn't you?" she finally croaked.

"I did," Scott insisted. "I asked him how he was."

"Oh, really? 'Cause all I heard was, 'Hey, hi . . . duh . . . ah.'"

Scott turned red. "Yeah, well, at least I said something. You were afraid to even talk to him."

Rebecca took a deep breath and nodded. "You're right. I was." She slowly turned to her little brother, feeling very uneasy and very concerned. "And maybe . . . maybe you should be too."

~

That evening Rebecca and Mom got ready for the concert while Scott played with his laptop computer.

"You'd better hurry and get ready, Scotty," Mom called from the other room. "We've got to leave in fifteen minutes."

"I *am* ready," he replied, keeping his voice calm. "Hey, Beck, I'm checking out The Scream's Web site. You should see it. The whole thing comes out of this huge skull."

"Why am I not surprised."

"What do you mean you're ready?" Mom yelped as she stepped into the room and stared at Scott's attire: a worn, torn sweatshirt, dirty jeans, and beat-up gym shoes.

"This is what you're *supposed* to wear to the concert," Scott explained in his most patient voice. "This is what *everyone* will be wearing. Except you and Rebecca."

"Really?" Mom asked in surprise. "But you . . . you look . . . so . . . destitute."

"'Destitute at the Institute.'"

"What?"

"That's a Scream song. You know, 'Destitute at the Institute, but alive in my mind.'"

Mom grimaced. "This is going to be a difficult evening for me, isn't it?"

Scott nodded. "Yes, Mom. I imagine it will be."

She sighed slowly. "All right. You can wear everything but the sweatshirt."

"Mom!" Scott protested.

"It stinks."

"But . . . it's the coolest thing I've got."

"Well, I want you to take it off."

Rebecca joined the conversation. "Mom, the sweatshirt is the focus of his entire outfit. Right, Scott?"

He tossed her a grateful look. "Yeah . . . exactly . . . what she said."

Mom nodded. "I see. And I still say it stinks. Literally. It smells because he hasn't washed it in a month. So . . . change it."

"All right," Scott finally conceded, mostly because he was more interested in what was happening on his computer than in continuing the conversation. "I've got a message coming in."

In the lower left-hand corner of the screen was a blinking yellow *Z*, signaling that an E-mail message was coming through. Scott had created the little *Z* symbol and programmed his computer so that it would be displayed whenever an E-mail message arrived. He would have liked to make the symbol come on only when the message was from Z, but Z's address was always changing. That was part of the mystery of Z . . . the person they had never met but who always seemed to know what they were doing. And sometimes even what they were thinking.

"Hey, it's Z," Scott called as he clicked on the *Z* symbol and the message appeared. "Check it out."

Rebecca joined him. Together the two read silently:

Greetings:
Hope you enjoy the hotel. I have two pieces of information.
1. Your mission is Mike Parsek. He is a pastor's son, but he has not communicated with his father for several years. He knows the truth from his childhood, but he's in over his head. He has no concept of the danger he's in.

2. Beware of Tommy Doland.

Rebecca felt a chill as she read the warning. Her eyes dropped to the bottom of the screen, where Z had written a brief Scripture. It wasn't long, but it was enough to remind her of the seriousness of their task:

"Watch out for attacks from the Devil, your great enemy. He prowls around like a roaring lion, looking for some victim to devour. Take a firm stand against him, and be strong in your faith."
1 Peter 5:8-9

Scott didn't seem to even see the warning or the verse. Instead, he pointed his finger to the number *1* on the screen. "See?" He smiled smugly. "I told you you should've talked to Parsek."

Becka shrugged. "What makes Z think these people will listen to us anyway?"

"Not 'these people,'" Scott corrected. "Mike Parsek. And I'd say by the way he scoped you out earlier that he'd be willing to listen to anything you say."

Rebecca's face flamed. She turned quickly, grabbed her coat, and headed for the door. Scott snapped off the computer and followed, smiling. Being a pesky little brother definitely had its advantages at times.

The Los Angeles Forum held about twenty
thousand people, and it was jam-packed. But
it wasn't the size of the crowd that bothered
Rebecca. It was the attitude. Everyone in the
place was angry.

Actually, beyond angry.

Most of them seemed ready to explode.
Everyone was huddled together in little
packs, scowling at anyone they didn't know
and acting up with everyone they did. It was
the most explosive group of people Rebecca
had ever seen under one roof.

And there are twenty thousand of them. All here.

From the expression on Mom's face,
things seemed equally bizarre to her. She
still hadn't gotten past the dress code.
Scott's comment about torn sweatshirts and
faded jeans had been an understatement,
but Becka hadn't had the heart to tell Mom
that. Now Mom's mouth gaped open at what
she saw all around them. . . .

One guy had three safety pins in his left
eyebrow. Another had one through his nose.
And one girl, clad all in leather, had four
Scream buttons pinned to her lower lip.

This was definitely not Mom's kind of
place.

"I had no idea that it'd be this . . . this . . .
bad!" she shouted as they made their way

toward their seats. "Maybe I should have stayed at the hotel."

"You can go back if you want, Mom!" Scott shouted. "We can probably find a ride."

To Mom's credit, her response was immediate. "Forget that thought, young man," she said firmly. "Now that I've seen what this is like, you definitely aren't going to be here without me."

Scott sighed. "Now you're sounding like a mom again."

Mom shook her head. "I'll be glad when this thing is over."

As they took their seats, Rebecca felt the tension in the air grow even more intense. The band was late in starting, and that made the crowd even rowdier. Then:

WHAM! WHAM! BOOOOOOOOM!

The explosions came from the stage, and the crowd began to roar. The show was about to start. As the curtain rose, the spotlights came on, bathing a huge skull in reds, blues, and yellows.

"Army of the night,
Not afraid to fight!"

The bright spots lit Tommy Doland. He screamed into the microphone as the guitar wailed and the bass and drums pounded the beat. Everyone in the crowd was on their feet, screaming.

Everyone but Becka. She couldn't explain it, but she felt so sick she had to sit down.

"What's the matter?" Mom shouted.

"Nothing," she replied. "It's just my stomach again. I'll be OK."

"Maybe it was something you ate," Mom shouted.

Rebecca nodded, but she knew it wasn't that kind of stomach trouble. She'd felt this before. It was the way she always felt when she encountered the demonic. And looking up at the stage, at Doland's eyes blazing as he shrieked the song, Rebecca knew with sudden certainty that the skulls and other symbols of satanism were far more than props.

There was something very real—and very frightening—going on here.

4

The intensity of the crowd built and subsided in perfect rhythm with the music and pacing of the show. As the band neared the end, it was one climax after the other, with each new one topping the last. By the time Mike Parsek launched into his famous drum solo, the crowd had been driven to a feverish pitch.

More and more effects were released. Two large fog machines at each end of the stage began to shoot out a mist that quickly enshrouded the bottom three feet of the stage. But Rebecca's eyes were drawn away from the fog . . . to the huge dragon cannon. So far it had remained a silent yet ominous presence. With firepots and other effects cutting loose all night from unseen places, one couldn't help but wonder what this big machine might do when fired. From her seat in the third row, Rebecca could see the top of the cannon rising just above the fog.

It had begun to vibrate.

She felt the urge to pray. *That's silly*, she thought to herself. *I'm not wasting energy worrying about some special effect. It's what the band wants. To freak people out. To make them think there's real danger when everything is under control.*

Still, the dragon cannon bothered her. And the harder Mike played, the more it vibrated, as if it was preparing to fire. Rebecca looked to Scotty, but he was watching Doland, plainly enthralled with the show.

Several times throughout the night, he and Rebecca had exchanged glances. It felt good to know that he was feeling something strange too. The only difference was that

Scotty wasn't about to let it spoil his good time.

"Scotty." Rebecca nudged him. "Let me see your binoculars for a minute."

She could tell he didn't appreciate the interruption, but he handed them to her anyway. She focused on the dragon cannon. It was definitely vibrating. Again she felt the urge to pray but dismissed it as a childish fear.

Then she saw something that made her blood run cold.

One of the large bolts holding the cannon in place had come loose. With every shake of the cannon, the bolt slipped more and more out of place. Any second now it would fall out completely!

Rebecca wasn't sure what that meant. She directed the binoculars to the opposite side of the cannon. . . . The other bolt appeared to be staying in place. Her stomach began to churn as she wondered if she should do something, tell somebody.

Mike drummed faster, increasing the intensity of his solo. Scotty reached for his binoculars, but Rebecca held them tight. She stared at the bolt as it shook back and forth . . . and then it fell out and into the fog.

Now, with only one bolt holding the cannon, the great machine shifted slightly with each vibration. The icy fear gripping Rebecca grew as she realized the cannon was turning. *Oh, Jesus,* she prayed, no longer dismissing the urging as childish. *Jesus, protect them!* No one onstage appeared to notice, but the cannon was turning and pointing in an entirely different direction.

She felt Scotty tapping her on the shoulder, but she wasn't about to give the binoculars back. As the drum solo reached a new crescendo, the cannon shook and vibrated even more.

It was about to fire!

And the more it vibrated, the more it turned, until it was pointing directly at the band. More specifically, it was aimed directly at the drummer, Mike Parsek!

God, don't let this happen! Don't let it end like this, before we even get a chance to talk with him. . . . Rebecca's lips moved as she prayed. Through the binoculars she saw a roadie crossing behind the band to some kind of control panel. A spark of hope surged through her.

Please, God, help him see that the cannon is loose. . . .

But the roadie didn't notice. Instead he flipped some switches on the control panel. The cannon shook even harder, but it could turn no farther.

It was pointing directly at Mike, and it was about to fire!

Rebecca watched the roadie press another button. A deep rumble began, louder than even Mike's drums. The cannon's firing mechanism ignited. She couldn't bear to look, but she couldn't bear to look away.

Mike reached the peak of his solo. He glanced to the side and suddenly saw the barrel pointing directly at him. But it was too late. The cannon ignited. . . .

But it did not fire.

Something had malfunctioned. Rebecca saw Mike shouting at the stagehand, frantically motioning for him to shut down the device. The stagehand leaped into action, and the cannon stopped vibrating.

Everyone was safe.

Rebecca knew why the cannon had failed to fire. Her prayer had been answered! Not exactly in the way she had prayed but answered nonetheless. And for that she offered up another prayer—this time a prayer of thanks.

~

Before the final note of the show was finished, Scott was already on his feet. He knew what they had to do. "Let's hurry up and get backstage."

"They just got done, Scotty," Rebecca said. "Shouldn't we give them a few minutes?"

"Are you kidding? In a few minutes there will be a hundred people in front of us trying to squeeze their way in." He glanced toward the door closest to the stage. Already scores of kids were lining up, hoping for a chance to glimpse one of the band members.

"But we have passes," Mom reminded him.

Scott nodded, trying to get them moving even as he talked. "I know, Mom. But you've got to show your pass to the burly guy who guards the door before he'll let you through. And before you can show your pass, you've got to get to the guy. And that'll be harder with every second we wait. Come on!"

"He's right." Rebecca nodded. "We'd better go."

The three of them made their way to the stage door. As they got close, Scott leaned over to Rebecca and whispered, "What about Mom?"

"What about her?"

"Maybe she shouldn't go back there with us. I mean, she doesn't fit in and . . ."

Rebecca looked at him blankly. It was obvious she wasn't going to help. "And what?"

"Well . . . you know." Scott fidgeted. "What are we going to say? 'Hi, Mike, we're Scott and Rebecca, and this is our mom'? Nobody brings their mom backstage."

Rebecca shrugged. "I don't think that's our decision, Scott."

"What do you mean?"

"Z is the one who sent the tickets and the passes. He must've wanted her to come along."

"What are you kids talking about?" Mom asked. "If it's what I think it is, you needn't bother to discuss it."

For an instant Scott thought Mom was going to be a sport and let them go by themselves. But then she added, "I'm *going* with you. Who knows what might be going on back there?"

Scott sighed. Great. Here he was getting to do practically the coolest thing in the world and his mom had to tag along. He felt like a ten-year-old.

It took a while to get through the horde of kids pressing toward the door—but not as long as Scotty had expected. And for that there was one very simple reason:

Mom.

"Excuse me, sir," she called out above the crowd. "We have backstage passes. Would you let us through, please?"

Scott knew that would never have worked if he or Rebecca had shouted it. Either the

guard would have thought they were lying, or
everyone in the crowd would have pounced
on them and tried to take the passes.

But with a mother in the lead, it was totally
different. Scott watched in amazement as the
sea of rough-looking, pierced, ringed, and tat-
tooed fans parted to let them through.

The big guy at the door eyed them suspi-
ciously—that was his job—but as soon as he
saw the passes, he opened the door for
them, and they stepped inside.

A party was going full blast. There were all
kinds of strange and interesting people, but
none of the band members.

Scott turned to a tall guy with long blond
dreadlocks. "Hey, excuse me . . . could you
tell me—," he began, but the guy walked by
without giving Scott a glance. Undaunted,
Scott turned to a girl who had a fake ruby in
her belly button and wore huge bell-
bottoms. "Miss, uh . . . could you tell me
where to find the band? We're supposed to
meet them and—"

But the girl was already laughing. "Don't
expect them for at least an hour. It's way
uncool for the star of the show to show up at
his own party any earlier."

With that, she moved along, heading for a
table of refreshments by the bar. Scott
shrugged and followed. In the center of the

table was a guitar made of salmon. The strings were some kind of cream cheese, and the tuning pegs were black olives on tooth-picks. It must've been pretty good because several people were scooping up crackers full of the stuff and wolfing them down. So, of course, Scott followed suit.

"Yuuuck!" he said loud enough to draw a couple of disapproving looks. "This stuff tastes terrible!"

Now, even that wouldn't have been so bad, but there were a couple of minor addi-tions. . . .

The first was when Scott tried to ralph up the offending bite of salmon and spit it out. The second was when he tried to get rid of the taste by eating some salsa. The *green* salsa. The *extra-hot* salsa.

He ran to the bar, hand over mouth, ges-turing to the bartender for something to drink. The man started to hand him a beer but caught Mom's disapproving look and changed it to a Coke. It didn't matter to Scott . . . as long as it was cool and wet. *Any-thing* to put out the fire.

By the time he gulped down the drink, Scott was aware of all the people staring at him. At least a dozen, maybe more. He turned to Rebecca and whispered, "What are they looking at? We're at a backstage party, for cryin' out loud. Everything should be cool here. I mean, *look* at these people! Are you telling me you still have to do things a certain way or people stare?"

Rebecca sighed. "I think it's called having manners."

Before Scott could fire off a classy come-back, the room broke into applause. He turned to see the band joining the party.

They wore different clothes than they had worn on stage, but their outfits were just as outrageous. Tommy Doland headed straight for the bar, where he ordered a double shot of whiskey, gulped it down, and then ordered a beer.

Scott turned and stared. Tommy Doland, the lead singer from The Scream, was less than five feet away from him! Amazing. Then, to top it off, Doland turned and actually looked at him!

He noticed me! Scott thought. *He's going to speak to me. We're going to become friends!*

Doland stared at him a long moment before finally speaking. "Get out of here, kid. You're bothering me."

Scott's mouth dropped open. Everyone stared at him as if he'd just thrown up in the punch bowl. It was a good thing there wasn't a punch bowl there, or he might have done just that.

And then, to make matters even worse, he saw Mom making a beeline for Doland. *Oh no,* he thought. *She's coming over to defend me!*

Fortunately, Mike intervened by walking directly up to Scott. "You must be Scott Williams. How are you? I'm Mike Parsek."

Scott tried to answer. He knew his mouth was moving, but he also knew nothing was coming out.

Mike continued. "Z is a friend of mine on the Net. He told me you'd be coming. How'd you like the show?"

"Uhhh . . . I . . . uh . . . good. . . . It was good." Scott knew he sounded like an idiot. He threw a glance at Doland. Fortunately, the guy had already forgotten him and was nuzzling up to some girl wearing an extra-large Scream T-shirt and heels so high she could hardly walk in them.

Scott looked back to Mike and saw that the drummer had turned to Rebecca. "You must be Rebecca," he said. "How'd you like the show?"

Caught totally off guard, Becka did a repeat of her brother's stellar performance: "Uhhh . . . I . . . uh . . . good. It was good."

Mike laughed. "I can see a strong resemblance between you two. And this must be your mother," Mike continued. "Hello, Mrs. Williams. How are you?"

Mom smiled warmly and shook Mike's hand. "Very well, thank you. I'm not used to that sort of show, but I found it . . . fascinating."

"Thank you," Mike replied with a smile.

"Who're your friends, Mike?" It was Doland, his arm draped over the girl in the T-shirt. He looked at Scott and smiled. Or was it a sneer?

"Lemme guess—they're from your daddy's church? Or maybe your Sunday school class?"

"Bug off, Doland," Mike replied. He then turned to Rebecca. "Nice to see you," was all he said before turning and walking away.

Doland snickered and also headed off.

Scott turned to Rebecca, disbelieving. "That's it?"

"I guess so," Rebecca said, sounding as disappointed as he felt.

Scott shook his head. "So much for the world of rock 'n' roll." How was he going to tell the guys back home about this? What a bust! "I guess we should go."

Rebecca agreed. "I guess we've done enough damage here for one night."

~

"Do you think going to that concert was a bad idea?" Rebecca asked Mom. Scott had gone for a late-night swim in the hotel pool, leaving Becka and Mom alone.

"No, honey," Mom answered.

"But the people," Rebecca continued. "Most of them were so weird . . . and mean."

"Some of them were nice."

"One of them," Rebecca corrected pointedly. "Part of me wants to get away from this place as fast as I can, but another part is saying that I should stop judging these people and try to help them. I must be crazy. I mean, these guys have the biggest-selling album in the country, and I'm supposed to think they actually need *my* help?"

Mom smiled. "Maybe they do. Money doesn't give you peace . . . and it certainly doesn't get you to heaven. That boy Mike is a good boy. I could tell that just talking to him. But he's mixed up with some pretty rough people. I can see why Z thinks he might get hurt."

"So, what am I supposed to do?" Becka sighed. "Run away from the bad stuff . . . or stick around and try to fix it?"

"I guess that depends upon what the Lord is telling you."

"What do you mean?"

"The Bible says we are to flee evil."

"That's right," Becka agreed.

"But it also says we are to help people, to

bring light into the darkness. The trick is to
know what God wants you to do . . . and
when to do it. If you find your light growing
dim because you're getting caught up in the
world, then you should flee. But if your light
is shining bright, then maybe you should
stick around for a while and see if you can
light up the place."

"And how am I supposed to know the difference?" Becka asked.

Mom took a deep breath and slowly let it
out. "I guess that's between you and God
again, isn't it?"

Rebecca nodded. As usual, Mom was right.

Twenty minutes later Becka was out on the
balcony, all alone, staring out at the twin-
kling lights of the Los Angeles night.

"Dear Lord, things are really weird this
time around. I mean, I know you want us to
reach out to these guys. I know you love
them as much as you love me. But . . . how
do you do it, Lord? How do you wade
through a mud hole to help someone without getting muddy yourself? I really need
your wisdom, Lord. I need to know what you
would have me do. . . ."

Becka paused for a moment, then continued. "I guess, to be honest, Lord, I really

need your heart, too. I mean, all I see when I look at these guys is something I want to avoid. So help me see them, *really* see them, with the love you have for them. Thank you, Jesus. Amen."

She opened her eyes, suddenly aware that she felt better. Not because she had an answer. The fact was she was as clueless as when she'd started. But she felt better all the same because she knew that, at the right time, the answer would come. And that was enough.

~

The Scream was back onstage before a packed auditorium as Mike blazed through his drum solo. Once again the great cannon began to vibrate as it prepared to fire. Only this time it was not disguised as a dragon. This time it was much bigger and far more ominous.

Rebecca sat in the audience cheering, when suddenly her expression turned to horror. A gnarled, twisted hand, more animal than human, came out from behind the curtain and moved the giant cannon until it was again pointed at Mike.

But he didn't seem to notice it. He just kept playing, getting closer and closer to the climactic moment.

Rebecca screamed, but he didn't hear her. No one heard her.

And then it happened. Mike went into his final crashing pattern, and suddenly the flames shot from the huge cannon, completely engulfing him. He stood up, staggered, and fell to the stage. He was on fire, writhing in agony, rolling this way and that, trying to extinguish the flames. But nothing worked. Finally his eyes met Rebecca's. He reached out his burned hands. His charred lips muttered something. She couldn't hear the words, but she knew what he was saying all the same.

"Help . . . me. Help. . . . Please, help. . . ."

Rebecca sat bolt upright, her chest heaving, her face bathed in sweat. She grappled for the light switch and turned it on. She was in the hotel room, in bed. She pressed a trembling hand to her clammy face, trying to still her shaking and slow her pulse rate. The dream had been intense. But at least she had her answer. She would stay. Mike needed her to stay.

It made no sense—not as far as she could see—but as long as there was a chance she could help, she would remain.

5

When Rebecca opened her eyes the next morning, the first thing she saw was Scott eating a bowl of cereal at the foot of her bed. And the first thing she heard was: "You know something, Sis, Frosty Flakes taste even better from room service than they do from the box."

Rebecca looked at him through sleep-swollen eyes. "You woke me up to tell me that?"

"Not just that," Scott said. "I also wanted to tell you about my plan."

Rebecca sighed. "This should be good."

"No, listen. I've got an idea."

"You always do."

"Let him talk, honey," Mom called out from the other room.

"OK," Rebecca mumbled, "so talk."

"All right, here's what we do. We check out of this fancy hotel and cash in the rest of the vouchers Z sent us for housing. Then we check in to a cheaper hotel and spend the money at Disneyland."

Rebecca rolled her eyes. "That's your plan?"

"It's better than going home. Or staying in this fancy-schmancy place and not being able to do anything else."

"I think we should stay where Z wants us to stay," Mom said, coming into the room. "And I do have a little extra money, so maybe later we could spend a day at Disneyland."

But Scott wasn't satisfied. "A day? I bet we could score enough on those vouchers to be there the rest of the week. Besides, Z only wanted us to stay here because this is where the band was staying while they got ready for their big cable-TV show. And now that we're not seeing the band anymore, what's the point? I mean, this place is expensive. And for what . . . those little chocolates they leave on your pillow after they make the bed?"

"What chocolates?" Rebecca and Mom asked in unison.

Scott turned sheepish. "The ones I ate yesterday . . . all three of them."

They were interrupted by a knock at the door.

"I'll get it," Rebecca said. "It's probably the maid with more chocolates. I want to be sure I get some this time."

But it wasn't the maid. When she opened up the door, she found Mike Parsek standing there. And instead of chocolates, he was holding a rose. "Hi," he said, smiling at a very shocked Rebecca. "This is for you."

Rebecca couldn't say a word. All she could think about was her morning hair . . . her morning face . . . her morning everything.

Fortunately, Mom came to the rescue. "Mike, how nice to see you. Why don't you come in for a while?" She nudged the dumbfounded Rebecca aside to let Mike enter the room.

"OK . . ."

After another embarrassed pause, Mom

came to the rescue again. "So, how did you find our room number?"

"Oh, Z gave it to me. I found it in my E-mail this morning."

"Cool," Scott chirped.

"Anyway, I just came by to see if Rebecca would maybe like to go out for lunch."

At first Rebecca was astonished, then flattered, and finally a little bugged. "I appreciate the invite, Mike, but . . ."

"But what?"

Rebecca shrugged. "I don't know. Could I ask you one question first?"

Mike nodded. "Fire away."

"Why did you leave like that? Last night. I mean as soon as Tommy Doland came over, you walked away without hardly saying a word."

"Ah." He nodded.

"And now you show up here with a rose and everything. I mean, I'm flattered, but . . . what's going on?"

"That's a good question," Mike answered, "but not an easy one. Let's just say that Tommy Doland is not someone you want to know."

"You acted like it was you who didn't want to know us," Rebecca said.

Mike nodded. "I know. It's just that . . .

well, sometimes he likes to make fun of my friends."

"That's pretty lame," Scott commented from across the room.

Mike looked at him, then nodded again. "You're right, it is. But if you give me another chance by going to lunch with me, maybe I can explain it better."

"OK," Scott said. "I'm willing to give it a shot."

Rebecca turned and glared at him. "I think he means me."

"Yeah." Mike grinned. "I mean Rebecca."

Scott snorted in disgust.

"Sorry, Scott." Mike shrugged. "But if you're going to be in town, we could sure use some extra help setting up for this big TV concert. Nothing too heavy. Just odds and ends. But we'd pay you ten bucks an hour."

"Ten bucks an—" Scott caught his breath and then tried again. Rebecca smiled as he did his best to respond with some semblance of being cool. "OK, I'll consider it . . . but only if you'll sign some things I brought from home for my friends."

"Sure. And if you don't mind, maybe I can throw in a signed copy of our latest album for you."

"You'd do that for—" Once again Scott's

voice cracked, and once again he fought to try to sound cool. "Yeah, I, uh, I think that would be all right."

There was no missing the chuckles all around the group.

Rebecca turned to Mom. "So, may I go to lunch with Mike?"

"Will you be eating in the hotel?" Mom asked.

Mike shook his head. "The hotel is too . . . popular. There's a nice café just down the block. I can give you my cell-phone number if you want."

"All right." Mom nodded. "Just don't be gone too long."

Mike nodded and wrote down the number. "I'll be back to pick you up around 11:30, Rebecca."

Later as Mike and Rebecca headed out the door, Mike turned back to Scott. "Listen, if you can be ready to work in a couple of hours, you can ride with me over to the hall. They're going to be miking the drums for a sound check."

"Great," Scott replied. "But . . . what about Doland? He didn't seem to like me very much last night."

"Just act like you've never met him. He was too stoned to remember anything about last night. That's how he always gets."

⁓

One floor above them was Tommy Doland's room. From the looks of things, there had been another wild party last night. As for Doland, he seemed to be passed out on the sofa, sleeping off a major drunk. But looks can be deceiving. Doland wasn't passed out. His eyelids were fluttering madly, and he was making strange little noises, more like grunts and growls than words. But one word did keep forming on his lips again and again.

One name . . .

Rebecca.

⁓

Rebecca and Mike were having lunch in a stylish Beverly Hills café. Rebecca's eyes widened when she saw the menu. Three bucks for a Coke? But Mike didn't seem to notice. Apparently he was used to this kind of place.

"So how do you like L.A.?" he asked her as they set the menus aside.

She shrugged. "It's OK, I guess, but I really haven't seen much of it."

Mike smiled. "Well, if you've got the afternoon free, we can fix that. After the sound check, I'll give you a personal tour, all right?"

Rebecca caught her breath. She was still having trouble believing Mike was so interested in spending time with her. But somehow she forced herself to stay calm and collected. "That'd be nice. 'Course I'll have to check with Mom first, but it sounds like a lot of fun."

When the waiter arrived, Rebecca ordered the shrimp scampi, but Mike ordered a plain old cheeseburger. As soon as the waiter had gone, Becka asked, "Are you sure this place is all right? I mean, we could still cancel our order and go somewhere else."

Mike looked surprised. "I thought you liked this place."

"Oh, I do. I just wondered if it might be too expensive."

Mike laughed. It was a nice, easy laugh, and even though she knew he was laughing at her, she didn't feel embarrassed. "Don't worry about the price," he said. "I told you I'd take you out to lunch."

"But . . . ," Rebecca stammered.

"But what?"

"But you only ordered a cheeseburger."

Mike grinned. "What's wrong with that?"

"Nothing. I just thought that maybe you ordered one to save money. . . . I mean, with all the fancy things on the menu here."

Mike laughed again. "I like cheeseburgers. More than all that fancy stuff. I mean, the other stuff is OK and everything, but once

you've tried all the different kinds of dishes
. . . well, cheeseburgers still taste the best."

"Oh, good . . ." Rebecca let out a sigh.
"I'm glad." She paused for a moment and
then continued. "You know, you really seem
different from the other guys in the band."
Mike continued to smile, but there was a
kind of sadness in his eyes as she went on. "I
mean, they seem so serious . . . kind of glum
or mad . . . especially Tommy Doland. Of
course, I don't know any of them, but . . ."

"They're OK. Jackie and Grant are pretty
good guys. At least they used to be. . . . To
tell you the truth, I don't hang around with
them much anymore." He shook his head.
"They spend too much time getting wasted,
and I'm just not into that."

"I'm glad," Becka said quietly.

Mike shrugged. "It didn't used to be so
bad. Drugs and booze were just a once-in-a-
while thing. But it seems like the longer
we've been together, the more they've tried
to tune everything out. I'm afraid most of it
has to do with Doland."

"What's he like?"

"Doland . . . he's pretty gone. Way over
the edge. I think Jackie and Grant know it,
too, but no one wants to confront him."

"Why not?"

"For one thing, he's the leader of the

band. As lead singer, he's the most recognizable. His voice is a big part of our sound. . . . Without him, there would be no band. And also . . . well, he's really hard to talk to these days. He just wants to do what he wants and nothing else."

"Sounds like my brother." Rebecca grinned.

Mike laughed again, and she was glad. Whenever Doland's name was brought up, Mike seemed so troubled. . . . It felt good to see him smile again. "No, Scott's not like Doland," Mike said. "Believe me."

"I don't know," Rebecca answered. "He sure wants his way all the time."

"Everyone's like that," Mike said. "Especially toward their brother or sister. I know. I've got three sisters, and they all drive me crazy."

Again they both laughed. Rebecca was beginning to like this guy, and she could tell he liked her. "When did you see them last? Your family, I mean."

Mike looked sad again. "It's been a couple of years. They're back in Arizona with my folks. My dad and I, we, uh . . . we don't get along too well."

"What's the problem?"

"Lots of stuff," Mike said. "He wants everything on the straight and narrow, and I'm just not wired that way. I like to experiment, to do different things. He likes everything in a box, nice and neat. His career, his family . . . and especially his son."

"I guess that could be hard," Rebecca agreed. "But I'm sure he still loves you."

Mike glanced up, clearly surprised at her remark. "Yeah . . . I suppose. But we can't live together, I can tell you that. I never could live up to his expectations."

"Why did Doland ask you if we were from your dad's church?"

Mike sighed. "Before my dad retired, he was a pastor. Doland likes giving me a hard time about it."

Rebecca frowned. "What's he got against pastors? Or churches?"

Mike looked out the window of the café for a moment and finally answered, "What's Tommy Doland got against pastors and churches? Nothing . . . except that he worships the devil."

In a dimly lit room, Tommy Doland sat at a table with three other people. They were all holding hands. A black candle sat in the middle of the table. A large bald man with a short black beard began to chant softly.

"Darkness and shadow hold back the

light; darkness and shadow hold back the light."

Doland and the other two people quietly took up the chant: "Darkness and shadow hold back the light; darkness and shadow hold back the light."

The chant lasted several minutes, growing louder and louder until it filled the room . . . until it filled their minds and bodies . . . until it was all they could hear or think or be: "Darkness and shadow hold back the light; darkness and shadow hold back the light."

Finally the leader raised his arms. The others fell silent and followed suit. Then the leader called out in a loud voice, "Overlord of the Western Hemisphere, Demon Prince of the city, what do you wish us to do with the intruder? What fate do you decree for this one who dares to challenge your authority over this carefully groomed project? What would you have us do with this person who has come to undermine our brother's efforts? What do you decree for Rebecca Williams?"

There was no response. Only silence. Then an unmistakable chill filled the room.

Suddenly the leader started to shake. The sound coming from him started as a deep rumble but grew into a vicious snarl. Tommy

Doland could feel his hands breaking out
into a sweat, but he kept his eyes clenched
tight, continuing to concentrate.

Slowly the snarl evolved into a voice, a terrifying, guttural voice. As it spoke, the flame
on the candle in the center of the table
began to waver. Suddenly the voice
screamed. They were only four words, but
they reverberated throughout the room for
a long, long time:

"DEATH TO THE GIRL!"

6

As soon as she returned from lunch, Rebecca asked Scott if she could use his laptop to contact Z.

"Wait until I get back, and I'll do it," Scott suggested.

"No, you'll be gone for a couple of hours. I need to talk to him now."

Scott hesitated. "I don't know. It isn't mine, you know. It's Darryl's, and he'd be pretty mad if you broke it."

Rebecca sighed. "I'm not going to play football with it. I just want to contact Z and ask him some questions about what Mike told me."

"All right," Scott said, handing her the laptop. "It's still got about an hour left on the charge, so you don't even need to plug it in."

"Thanks," Rebecca said, already typing on the keyboard.

"Whoa," Scott said, looking at his watch. "I'm supposed to be downstairs meeting Mike. Hope he holds the limo for me. See ya later."

"Bye . . . oh, Scott, stay away from Doland. I'm afraid he might be—"

But Scott was already out the door.

～

Scott bounded out of the elevator and into the lobby, where he could see the limo waiting. "Cool!" he shouted a little too loudly for the somewhat reserved atmosphere of the Beverly Hills hotel. Running was also frowned on, so Scott forced himself to slow to a fast walk as he headed toward the door.

"Hey! Where's the fire?" a voice called out behind him. Scott turned around to see Mike. "Wait up, Scott. Didn't think we'd leave without you, did you?"

"Uh, n-no," Scott stammered. "But who is 'we'?"

"Well . . ." Mike hesitated. "Doland wants to check out the effects unit. They repaired it after last night."

Scott was caught off guard. "Doland? But I thought—"

Mike cut him off. "Tommy, I want you to meet the newest member of our crew."

Scott hadn't noticed that Doland had been sitting near the door waiting all along. The guy looked like his mind was a thousand miles away as he stood up to meet them.

"Tommy," Mike said again as they reached the door, "this is Scott Williams. He's going to help us get ready for the show."

Suddenly Doland's eyes came into focus. Piercing. Intense. "Hello, Scott."

Scott swallowed nervously. "Hi . . . Tommy." He was relieved that Doland didn't seem to recognize him from last night's party.

But as they headed out of the hotel entrance, Doland turned and said, "So where's your lovely sister today? Upstairs? In the room . . . I presume?"

He said the last phrase in a singsongy voice, as if it were a rhyme he'd made up especially for the occasion. Scott could only stare, still nervous that Doland might remember him.

Doland said nothing, obviously waiting for an answer.

Finally, Scott said, "Yeah . . . I guess. She was using my laptop to contact . . ." He'd almost said Z but figured it was none of Doland's business. Why would he tell Doland anything?

Doland smiled that twisted smile of his. "Using your laptop, huh? Guess that's the story, *A* to *Z*."

He emphasized the *Z*, and with a cold chill, Scott wondered if it was just a coincidence or if Doland had somehow, someway, read his mind.

~

Rebecca had no problem getting through to Z. She was getting better at using the laptop all the time. She quickly filled Z in on what had happened so far, especially about her conversation with Mike.

What can I do to help Mike?

She waited a few moments, and then Z's reply came across the screen.

Get him away from Tommy Doland.

At first Rebecca figured she'd miscommunicated something. So she tried again:

*How can we do that? Doland's the lead
singer of the band.*

Z's answer was typically honest and straight
to the point.

Doland has willingly given himself over to the
devil. He will keep Mike from the spiritual
truth he needs.

Rebecca sat, puzzled. Slowly she typed:

*How can I ask Mike to quit the biggest thing
in his life?*

The answer returned quickly:

It was Christ who said, "How do you benefit if you
gain the whole world but lose your own soul in
the process? Is anything worth more than your
soul?" Without Christ there is no life. Everything
else will pass away.

Rebecca nodded. Z was right; she knew it.
But it didn't make it any easier.

The Scream is the hottest band in the country.

Of course she knew there was no compari-
son between a hot band and the God of the

universe, but she didn't know if she could get that across to Mike. For a moment she wondered if Z would even bother replying, but the response soon came.

Better to be the least within the kingdom of God than the greatest without.

Finally Rebecca typed out her greatest concern:

If Mike's father, a pastor, couldn't reach him, how can I?

The response was swift:

Maybe you can't, but you should try.

Rebecca answered:

But how? Maybe after we've known each other for a while, sure. But not yet.

Z's response appeared on the screen, and it filled Rebecca with dread:

Mike does not have that much time.

Becka remembered her dream of the fiery cannon and was suddenly terrified for her

new friend. But before she could type anything else, Z's final words appeared.

Must go. Do your best. And be careful. The devil
knows our weaknesses and uses them against
us. Remember that people are praying for you. Z

Becka didn't fully understand the last part,
but she was so overwhelmed she didn't care.
Instead, she did what she usually did when
she was overwhelmed. She prayed. She
guessed Z had meant Mike's family when he
said there were a lot of people praying, but
she figured it wouldn't hurt to add one more.

~

Scott was amazed at how much bigger the
auditorium looked when no one was there.
"It's like you could put my whole hometown
in here!"

Mike smiled, then turned to a scraggly
looking guy with a bandaged hand and several sores on his face. "Scott, this is Billy
Phelps. He's our stage manager. He got hurt
at the San Francisco concert. But he's doing
better now, right, Billy?"

Billy grinned. "Right."

"He'll show you what you need to do,"
Mike finished.

"Hey, Scott," Billy drawled with a slight southern accent. "You ready to rock?"

Scott shrugged. "Yeah . . . I guess."

Billy nodded. "All right. You can start with that bucket of empty whiskey bottles over there."

Scott turned to see a large tub filled with empty bottles.

"Take 'em over to that sink back there, and wash 'em out real good."

Scott nodded. "OK. Then what?"

"Then come see me. I'll be tinkering with the lights somewhere around the stage. Get me when you're done, and we'll fill 'em up."

"OK," Scott agreed, wondering why they wanted to reuse the bottles. *Oh, well,* he thought. *Guess it doesn't matter. I'm now part of the world of rock 'n' roll.*

～

Tommy Doland watched the boy talking to Billy and Mike, feeling the rage build inside him. He leaned over the control panel at the edge of the stage. So Rebecca Williams was sending her brother into battle as well, was she? Well, that was just fine. He could handle them both. And handle them he would.

~

After setting the levels for the drums, Mike returned to join Rebecca. She'd wanted to see a bit more of Los Angeles, and he had wanted to spend more time with her. Now they stood at the famous intersection of Hollywood and Vine and looked up at the Capitol Records tower just down the street. When Rebecca looked to the left, she could just make out Mann's Chinese Theater, where the footprints of all the great stars—everyone from Clark Gable and Marilyn Monroe to Jack Nicholson and Michelle Pfeiffer—were in cement.

It should've been an exhilarating experience, but it wasn't. The Hollywood of old was long gone. Off to Rebecca's right were overpriced souvenir shops and topless bars. The street was busy all right, but no movie stars were to be seen. Instead, the sidewalks were filled with drug addicts and prostitutes. There were tourists here and there, but there were far more homeless people. And it cut Rebecca to the quick to see many kids her age—and some even younger—among them. Young people from around the country had come out to Hollywood thinking they'd escape their boring hometown life . . . only to find themselves caught up in an urban nightmare. For them, the street of dreams was nothing but a street of pain.

She felt a sense of relief when they headed for the limo. Mike had the driver take them past the fancy mansions of Beverly Hills and then out to the Venice Beach boardwalk. The afternoon was growing more perfect by the moment.

They hadn't talked much about The Scream. Rebecca was anxious to ask more questions after what she'd learned from Z, but she suspected the subject would upset Mike, and she didn't want to do that. Everything was too perfect.

Half an hour later they were having ice-cream sundaes at an outdoor shop in the Century City mall. The big office building towered over them, and the mall was crowded with busy executives.

"See that guy over there?" Mike nodded to the right.

Rebecca turned to see a short man dressed in an expensive business suit, Italian sunglasses perched on his nose, walking hurriedly through the mall. Three taller men wearing similar suits and sunglasses were trying their best to keep up with him.

"That's Michael Ovatti, the agent," Mike said. "Some people think he's the most powerful guy in the entertainment business."

"Who are the other three guys?"

"Dunno. Underlings probably. He's got a zillion of them, or so they say."

"Do they all try to dress like he does?"

"Sure," Mike said. "And walk and talk like he does too."

Rebecca laughed. "That's crazy."

"You got that right," Mike said with a grin. "Now, what do you want to do next?"

"Watch the sun go down into the ocean," Rebecca said before she could catch herself.

Mike smiled. "All right, one sunset coming up. But after that, I need to get you back to the hotel. I told your mom we wouldn't be out too late."

It wasn't until they were back in the limo, heading toward Zuma Beach, that Becka finally worked up the courage to talk about the band.

"Mike . . . can I ask you something?"

Mike nodded. "Shoot."

"What are you going to do about the band?"

He looked puzzled. "Do? What do you mean?"

"Well, I was thinking about what you said about Doland. About his worshiping the devil and stuff. Doesn't that worry you?"

Mike sighed and looked off into the distance. "Well, I used to think it was an act with

Doland . . . but not anymore. Sometimes it doesn't bother me at all. Other times . . ."

"What?" she prodded.

"Well, sometimes, like when everyone makes a big fuss over us . . . sometimes that bothers me."

"Why? I mean, you've worked hard for it."

Mike nodded. "We're a good band and all, but there are lots of good bands. Sometimes I just . . . I guess I feel funny about the band's success because I'm not sure where it came from."

Rebecca gulped. She had a hunch where this was going.

Mike continued, "In the beginning, the black magic and devil stuff were more of a gimmick than anything we believed in. We even used to make fun of it. But it kept growing somehow, and then . . . it just got out of control. Especially with Doland. And now, it's like the band isn't even in charge anymore."

"What do you mean?"

Mike shrugged, looking uncomfortable as the limo pulled into the beach parking lot. "I don't know. I'm probably just superstitious. All the guys say I am."

"That's just because you believe in something—" Becka stopped in midsentence, not sure if this was the right thing to say. "Or . . .

at least you *did* believe in something . . . at
one time."

Mike laughed. "Yeah, I guess that's one
way of putting it."

Two minutes later they were sitting on the
hood of the limo, watching the sun sink into
the ocean. Becka could not have asked for a
better day. A great lunch, a tour of L.A. in a
limo, and now a perfect sunset beside a
great guy.

She took a deep breath and slowly let it
out. "This is so beautiful," she said. "I always
try to take time to watch the sunsets at
home."

"I bet it's even prettier where you live,"
Mike said.

"I don't know. It all depends on where
you are at the moment."

Mike turned and looked into her eyes.
"And who you're seeing it with?"

Rebecca felt her stomach do the slightest
flip-flop, and a warmth rushed to her
cheeks. "Yes . . . that too."

He hesitated a moment longer before
leaning toward her for a kiss. She leaned forward too. Then at the last second she
blurted out, "So, are you going to tell me
what you meant by feeling like the band
wasn't in charge anymore?"

Mike stopped and looked at her. "You

sure have a strange way of communicating sometimes, Rebecca Williams."

She gave a nervous smile.

Mike turned to stare at the sunset again. "All I meant was that sometimes things feel so out of control that it's like . . . it's as if someone, or some*thing,* else is calling the shots. I don't know, but I think Doland is into some pretty weird stuff and . . . somehow that effects all of us."

"Then why don't you quit?"

Mike laughed. "Are you serious?"

Rebecca nodded. "Sure, if it's the only way you'll be free of Doland."

"Quit the band?!" Mike's voice carried an edge of irritation. "No way. I worked my whole life for this. I'm never quitting the band."

Rebecca felt miserable. "Look, I'm sorry. I didn't mean to upset you. It's just that, well, I've seen people fool around with demonic stuff . . . and it can get pretty dangerous. I mean, something awful could happen . . . and I . . ."

He was looking at her again.

For a moment she forgot what she was saying.

". . . I don't want anything . . ."

He began leaning toward her.

". . . awful to happen to . . ."

His lips found hers. For an instant Rebecca

melted. She kissed him back. Passions rose. Mike's arms came around her, and he held her firmly, kissing her harder. Rebecca knew she should pull away. For an instant she even thought of Ryan back home. How would she feel if he was kissing some other girl? Then came the thought of her promise to Mom about never letting herself get into a compromising situation with a boy.

Yet, in spite of all that, she let the kiss continue. It grew in intensity until all she could think of was *Mike, Mike, Mike. . . .*

Then another thought came to mind: *"The devil knows our weaknesses and uses them against us."*

Startled, she stiffened. Then, mustering all of her will, she pulled away.

Mike looked at her, a little confused, a little hurt.

She wanted to explain herself but didn't know if she could. Was this the weakness Z had warned her about? Something the enemy would use against her? Part of her knew that when you're dealing with the devil, things are rarely what they seem. And the pull of Mike's passion—and her own—had been surprisingly strong.

She let out a small breath of air. "I've, uh, I've got to get going," she finally managed. "Mom will be worrying."

Mike slowly nodded. "Sure . . . and I've got a band meeting I should get to. We've got to iron out the final plans for tomorrow's telecast. It's the biggest thing for us yet. A national broadcast. It's going to be a real blast."

Rebecca nodded. But as they slid off the hood and started back into the limo, all she could think of was her dream from the night before—the one with the cannon exploding—and Mike's words . . . *"It's going to be a real blast."*

7

The next morning Rebecca tried to contact Z again. She had wanted Scott to join her, but he was busy listening to the latest Scream CD on his headphones. "If I'm going to be a part of the band, then I need to be more familiar with their music," he had shouted over the music.

"You're *not* part of the band," Rebecca shouted back. "You're just helping them set up for one show."

Scott removed the headphones. "That's all you know. First of all, when we in showbiz refer to the 'band,' we mean the entire organization that makes the thing happen. The agents, producers, label execs, manager, road manager, and crew—that last part includes me. As for this being my only show, Billy already said that he wished he had someone like me around all the time."

Becka shrugged. "So?"

"So that's exactly the kind of thing they say before they offer you a regular gig."

Rebecca tried not to laugh. "A regular gig? Don't you think you ought to finish school first?"

Scott pointed his index finger at Rebecca and then flipped his hand over in a quick gesture.

"What does that mean?" she said. "Or do I want to know?"

"It means, 'Have it *your* way, burger brain.' It's a band thing. Billy does it whenever the hall manager or the security guys hassle him. I think it's pretty cool."

Rebecca sighed. "I think it's pretty stupid. You've only been working for them one day, and you're already all caught up in this . . . band stuff."

"You're so uncool, Rebecca."

"And you're even more of an idiot than usual."

"I am *not* more of an idiot," Scott snapped as he put the headphones back on. "I'm just the same as I've always been."

Rebecca shook her head in amusement as she turned back to the computer. She wanted to talk with Z, to tell him he'd been right about the enemy using her weaknesses against her. She was falling for some guy she was supposed to be helping. And instead of making things better, she was afraid she was only making matters worse.

Then there was Scotty. He was getting caught up too, but instead of romance it was the band's fame—all the glitz and the hype. Yessir, there was definitely a battle going on. But one like they'd never fought before. Instead of in-your-face warfare, everything was cool and good and very, very seductive. In fact, when she thought about it that way, she realized the weapons being used against them in this encounter were actually more dangerous than in some of the other fights they'd faced. Because in this encounter, all of the enemy's weapons were things they wanted.

The E-mail symbol on the laptop began flashing, and Becka brought the message up on the screen. But it wasn't from Z. It was from Ryan:

Hello, Becka:
Hope you guys are doing OK. I miss you
a lot, but I guess I have to learn to put
my needs aside when you're doing important
stuff like this. Who knows what good effect this
kind of thing can have on others. I guess that's
the great thing about being a Christian.
All we have to do is say yes to God, and he does
the rest. All you and Scott had to do was be
willing to go to L.A., and now God's leading
you step-by-step the rest of the way.
I just wanted to let you know that I'm praying
for you guys, and I can't wait until you get back.
Love,
Ryan

It was all Rebecca could do to swallow back the lump in her throat. Ryan was the closest thing to a boyfriend she had ever had. And though she still didn't feel comfortable with that term, he had always treated her wonderfully. Now, here he was, trying to encourage her to let God use her to help others, saying he was praying for her . . . and she had practically dumped him for some guy she hardly even knew. If she had felt bad about kissing Mike before, she felt terrible about it now.

And it was these exact feelings that helped her decide what to do next.

"Scott, I want to go to rehearsal with you today."

Scott was in his own world with the headphones on over his ears and his eyes closed.

"He can't hear you with those things on," Mom said as she passed by. "You'll have to get his attention."

Rebecca agreed. Seeing a pencil eraser on the table nearby, she grabbed it and threw it at him, hitting him square in the forehead.

Scott's eyes popped open, then glared at her. "Hey! What was that for?" he demanded, jerking off his headphones.

"I was just trying to get your attention."

"Why didn't you just use a club?"

"I couldn't find one," she countered. "Listen, I want to go to rehearsal with you today."

"We're not rehearsing. We're recording," Scott replied. "You'll just get in the way."

Rebecca shook her head. "I'm not going to help. I'm going because I need to talk to Mike. What time are they sending the car?"

"Two o'clock," Scott replied. "But you'd better not bother Mike when he's recording."

"He won't get mad at me," Rebecca said confidently.

"It's not Mike I'm worried about. Doland's the one who'll get upset. He doesn't like distractions."

Rebecca paused, and for the briefest second she considered not going. Her stomach was already churning. The last thing she wanted was a confrontation with Doland. In fact, she dreaded seeing Doland at all.

But it had to be done.

~

The band had gone over early, so Scott and Rebecca were the only ones in the limo that afternoon. Scott wore his best torn T-shirt and torn jeans. In fact, they were *new* torn jeans. "Scott, are those your new jeans?" Rebecca asked incredulously. "Tell me you didn't tear holes in your new jeans."

"Don't tell Mom, OK?"

"I won't have to. She'll figure that out herself. Don't you think you're taking this band thing a little too far?"

Scott scowled and looked out the window. Even though they teased each other constantly, they had always been close. They had to be after all they'd been through together. But something was happening to Rebecca's little brother. In the past forty-eight hours

he seemed to have begun slipping away—
growing more and more distant, more and
more into himself. She knew it had to do
with the band—with the subtle deception he
was buying into—but she also knew that if
she brought it up, he wouldn't listen.

There was, however, Someone who would
listen.

God, please protect us, she prayed. *It feels like
we're in over our heads on this one. I know you
say when we're weak, you're strong. Well, we've
sure got plenty of weaknesses showing up this
time! Please be there for us. Protect us. Show us
what to do.*

As soon as they got out of the car, the limo
drove off, leaving them standing outside a
plain-looking brick building. "Are you sure
this is the place?" Rebecca asked. "It looks
like a warehouse."

"This is the address Billy gave me," Scott
said. "I think they like to keep it low-key on
the outside so people won't know about all
the expensive equipment inside."

The door was locked, and a small sign said
Ring Buzzer. Rebecca pushed the buzzer.
Nothing happened.

"Maybe we should've called first," Scott
said after a minute.

Suddenly they heard a whirring sound.
Looking up, they saw a small camera tucked

away under the awning. It was slowly turning, and then the lens moved.

"What's that?" Scott said.

"It's a security camera," Rebecca replied.
"Very high tech. They're checking us out.
Wonder who's on the other end."

"Probably some jerk," Scott said.

Then a voice out of nowhere said, "Watch
who you're calling a jerk, jerk."

Scott blushed. "They can *hear* us!"

The voice spoke again. "Right you are,
dweeb boy. Lucky I know you're smarter
than you look."

"It's Billy!" Scott exclaimed.

"Right again," the voice said. "Come on in."

With that he buzzed the door open.
Inside, the place was completely different
than it looked from the outside. They
entered a large reception area with walls of
sleek black marble and a thick, plush black
carpet. The walls were covered with silver
and platinum records in black metal frames.
On them were names like Pearl Jam, Alanis
Morrisette, Aerosmith, Petra, and Boys II
Men.

"Wow!" Scott said. "Look at this. All these
people recorded here!"

Rebecca was also impressed. "Hey, here's
Jars of Clay. I love that band."

In the center of the room was a large

black marble-looking reception desk. To the left of the desk were three monitors displaying images from the security cameras at the three entrances to the building. To the right of the desk was a fancy phone system and an expensive-looking PC. And behind all this beautiful high-tech equipment sat the scraggly Billy Phelps.

"Howdy." Billy grinned. "Pretty cool place, eh?"

"I'll say," Scott replied. "Where are the guys?"

Billy pointed down the hallway. "Studio B. They're doing overdubs. But I brought some of your work with me."

"Work?" Scott asked.

Billy nodded and pointed toward a large tub of empty whiskey bottles and a couple of plastic jugs full of an orangish brown liquid. Scott nodded.

Becka cleared her throat. "Excuse me . . . but I came to see Mike."

Billy nodded. "I figured. You're Rebecca, right?"

She nodded back.

"They're in the middle of a take right now, but I'll get word to them in a minute that you're here."

Rebecca thanked him and crossed to

where Scott was filling the empty bottles. "What are you doing?"

"Yesterday Billy had me wash out these whiskey bottles. Today he wants me to fill them. . . ."

"Is that whiskey?" Rebecca interrupted, pointing at the plastic jugs from which Scott was filling the bottles.

"No," Scott replied. "That's just it. It's iced tea."

"Iced tea? Why would they want . . . Oh, I get it."

Scott waited, but Rebecca said nothing. Finally he sighed, "Well, then, explain it to me, will you?"

Rebecca shook her head in sad amusement. "Don't you get it? They want to strut around onstage, guzzling from these whiskey bottles like it doesn't bother them . . . which it doesn't since the bottles are really just full of iced tea."

"Can't give a good performance when you're drunk," Billy Phelps said, walking up behind them. "You can go in now, Rebecca. Right down the hall. Only make sure you don't enter when the red light is on."

~

As Rebecca headed down the hall, Scott turned to Billy. "I still don't get this whiskey thing," he said. "Why do the guys want people to think they're drinking a lot when they're not?"

"Part of the image, kid. The crowd expects that from a heavy-metal band. Part of the whole rock-'n'-roll mystique."

"What about the kids out there who think they should be imitating them by guzzling down booze?"

"Oh, well." Billy grinned.

Scott frowned. He didn't much like the answer.

"This stuff is big business, kid. Too much money on the line to blow something because of a few drinks."

"Doesn't sound very real to me," Scott said.

"It's not about real, Scott," Billy said. "It's about money."

Rebecca walked down the hall, which was also lined with gold and platinum records. On the left was a large, airtight, wooden door. Rebecca started to grab the handle, then stopped when she noticed the red light glowing above the door. Several seconds later it turned off, and she went in.

Inside the dimly lit studio, Mike, Jackie, and Grant stood near a long recording console just a few feet away. It looked like the equalizer section on Scotty's stereo, except it was about fifty times larger. Behind the board sat a bushy-haired guy with glasses, who was turning and tweaking various knobs as he listened with the others to the play-back of a vocal Doland had just recorded. Through a big picture window she could see Doland, listening to the playback from the vocal booth. As soon as she entered, Mike smiled and nodded to her.

Rebecca grinned back but instinctively pulled away from the window to where Doland could not see her.

"You guys are acting like a bunch of wimps about this fire-cannon thing," Doland shouted at the rest of the band through the monitor speakers. "We're letting the fans down. They come expecting a wild ride, and that means the whole ball of wax—fireworks and pushing the envelope."

"Sure," Jackie Vee spoke to him through the intercom. "But we've got to have this stuff double- and triple-checked. I'm not spending my life in jail because this stupid cannon of yours takes some guy's arm off in the tenth row."

Becka felt her stomach tighten. They were talking about the cannon. The same one that had nearly killed Mike earlier. The same one, only smaller, that she had

dreamed about—the one that had covered
Mike head to toe in flames as he desperately
reached out to her for help. The image of
his burned face and charred lips screaming
in agony was so vivid that for a moment
Becka actually thought she saw it. She closed
her eyes, and it went away. Unfortunately,
the topic of the cannon did not.

"The cannon will be fine. I told you that.
Billy looked at it. It'll be fine."

"What was wrong with it?" Mike asked.

"It came loose, all right?" Doland
snapped. "That stuff happens."

"What about the night Billy got hurt?"
Mike persisted. "What was wrong with it
then?"

"I don't know!" Doland was getting more
and more angry. "I'm not an expert on can-
nons. I just don't want to wimp out for the
big show, that's all. We're talking national
TV here, boys. A forty-million-plus audience.
Our biggest show ever."

"All right, all right." Jackie Vee raised his
hands. "Let's keep the cannon in."

Grant, the bass player, reluctantly nodded.
It was clear Mike didn't agree, but it was
equally clear he had just been outvoted.

That decision settled, they went back to
the music.

"That last take was great, Tommy." The

bushy-haired producer behind the recording board spoke into his talk-back microphone. "But I'd like to try another one if you can. Try holding back a bit on the second chorus so that it makes more of an impact on the last chorus when you cut loose."

"You want *more* on the last chorus?" Doland's voice through the monitor speakers definitely sounded offended.

"No, no," the producer replied. "I want the same there . . . just soften the second chorus so that the last one stands out more."

"That's what I said!" Doland snapped. "You want *more* on the last chorus. Just roll the tape, man."

"OK," the producer said, doing his best to keep the peace. "We're rolling."

As the song began, Mike took the opportunity to step over to Rebecca. "Hi," he whispered.

She smiled. "I hope I'm not interrupting anything."

"No, no. Doland just wants to sweeten up some of the vocals."

"Will he mind that I'm here?"

Mike shook his head. "With the bright lighting in his booth and the dim light in here, he can't even see you. Is everything OK?"

Becka took a breath. "Well . . . yes and no." *Here goes,* she thought. "Mike, I really have gotten to like you in these past few days, and I hope we stay friends for a long time, but—"

"Whoa!" Mike cut her off. "It's the 'let's just be friends' speech? Already? I didn't expect that for at least another week."

Rebecca smiled. "Sorry, Mike. It's just that there's this boy back home that I like and . . ."

Mike nodded. "And what?"

"And . . . well, I sort of got carried away last night on the beach. The sunset and all . . . and you. I was letting my emotions get the best of me."

"Some people call that love, Beck," Mike said, looking straight into her eyes.

For a moment Rebecca began to weaken, but Z's message and remembering what Ryan had written strengthened her. She continued, "I suppose, but I call it . . . well, I call it losing control. I mean, I'm flattered and everything, but I know what I want now, and . . . this isn't it."

A slight frown crossed Mike's face.

"Don't get me wrong," Rebecca continued. "It's attractive, but . . . I just, I just don't think I'm ready for a serious relationship."

"What do you call what you have with the boy back home?"

"We're friends," Rebecca answered. "Well, actually, a little more than friends. It's growing, but it's at a slow pace. And that's the way I like it."

"Does this mean you're not coming to the TV concert tonight?"

"I was hoping to, unless you'd prefer me not to come. I do consider you a friend, Mike. I suppose that sounds stupid, but I really do care for you that way. And . . ." She hesitated, unsure if she should go on but knowing she had to. "I've been worrying about you a lot."

"Me?" he looked surprised.

She nodded, but before she could continue Doland started singing his vocal. Everyone suddenly grew very quiet.

The lyrics had barely started before Rebecca felt that all-too-familiar chill running across her shoulders.

But it was more than just his voice.

Mike was right. Because the lights in the control room were much dimmer than in Doland's vocal booth, there was no way that he could see she was there. Yet as he sang, his eyes seemed to focus directly upon her. Gradually they filled with more and more hatred, glaring at her, boring into her . . . and definitely scaring her.

The song continued to build. Now Doland

seemed to be going into some sort of trance. Rebecca had seen similar expressions before. Too many times during encounters with demons. If she'd doubted before that Doland had turned control of his life over to someone or something, she was sure of it now. And whatever that something was, Rebecca was equally sure it was not good.

A better word would be . . . *evil.*

Soon Rebecca found herself doing what she always did when she became afraid. She prayed. Silently. But it wasn't a prayer for help. Instead, it was a quiet worshiping, a reminder to herself of God's great power: *Thank you, Lord. Thank you for your love, for your awesome—*

She'd barely started when Doland screamed. It was a hideous sound. Terrifying. A sound more animal than human— one that cried of deep rage and pain.

The producer scrambled to stop the tape. "Tommy! What's wrong?"

Even stronger chills ran through Rebecca as Doland, still unable to see her, pointed directly at her. His voice was low, guttural. *"Get her out of here!"*

"Who?" the producer asked. "Get who out, Tommy?"

Doland glared maniacally. *"Get her out now!"*

Rebecca looked up at Mike. Her mouth was bone dry. "He means me."

"But he can't even see you! How could he—"

"Trust me on this, Mike. He means me. Can we talk somewhere? It's really important we talk."

Mike nodded. "Sure. Let's go into the hall." As soon as they stepped into the hallway, he looked down at her intently. "What happened in there? How'd he know you were there?"

Rebecca took a deep breath and slowly let it out. "Mike . . . I think Doland's under some kind of . . . I think the devil has a stronghold inside of him."

"Whoa." Mike held up his hand. "Doland's weird and all, but he's not . . . possessed. I mean, I know the guy's a jerk, but—"

"He went nuts just now because I was praying."

Mike looked at her strangely. "Praying?"

Rebecca nodded. "I was praying when he went crazy."

"Don't be silly," Mike said. "Doland didn't know you were praying. He just doesn't like strangers there."

"But he couldn't see me. You said so yourself."

The reply caught Mike off guard. "Look, I know Doland's weird sometimes, but—"

"Doland is more than weird. And it's almost all the time. You know that better than I do." She held his eyes, and after swallowing again, she continued, "It's dangerous for you here, Mike. You know the truth. You know what Doland's about. And if you keep refusing—"

"Look, Rebecca." Mike cut her off. There was no missing the anger in his voice. "If you don't want to date me, fine. But don't preach to me, either."

Suddenly Doland threw open the door to the studio. "What is *she* doing here?!"

"She's . . . she's my friend," Mike said.

Doland yelled loud enough for the rest of the band to hear. "I'm out of here until Mike's through messing around with the chicks! I'll be in the bar next door."

He started toward Becka, and she braced herself, but he did not touch her. Still, even as he passed, his glare was so intense that she found herself taking a step back.

There was something evil there. She knew it beyond the shadow of a doubt.

8

Doland stormed out of the hall of the studio, letting the door slam behind him.

Mike looked at the ground and slowly shook his head. "Well, that about does it for today. I'd say his concentration is definitely blown." He turned to Becka. "Listen, you want a ride back to the hotel?"

"What about Scotty?"

"What about me?" Scott asked as he strolled up with Billy and Jackie.

"We'll take him home," Billy offered.

Rebecca hesitated. "OK . . . I guess we'll see you back at the hotel, then."

"Sounds good to me," Scott said. Without another word, he turned and followed Billy and Jackie out the door.

As soon as they were in the parking lot, Jackie Vee turned to Scott and asked. "So, are you coming to the preshow party?"

"Sure," Scott said without thinking. "Where is it?"

"House up in the hills," Jackie replied. "Starts in a couple of hours. Probably be a little wild."

Scott knew something was wrong and that he shouldn't go. But the TV show would be in just a few hours, and after that his job would be over. Tomorrow he'd be back on the plane heading home, and the band would be just a memory. So before he could stop himself, he answered, "Sure, I'll be there."

～

In Mike's limo on the way home, Becka said another silent prayer. It was time to bring up the subject of the band again, and this time she hoped he'd understand. "Mike . . . I . . .

I want you to know something. It's only because I care about you that . . . that I think it's important you think about leaving the band."

Mike's eyes flashed anger. "You sound just like my father when you say that."

"Don't you think your father cares about you?"

"Sure he cares about me. But he wants to control my every move too."

"Isn't that just because he loves you?"

"You don't know him."

"No, I don't. But I do know that God still loves you."

Mike made a face. "Please . . ."

"Mike, don't confuse your feelings about your dad with your feelings about Jesus. Your father may have been a pastor, but he wasn't perfect. Christ's love is perfect. Don't turn your back on him."

Mike sighed. "I suppose now you're going to tell me that Jesus wants me to quit the band too?"

"Do you think Jesus wants you to sing songs that give glory to Satan?"

Mike shook his head. "Becka, that's just part of the show."

The car pulled into the hotel's parking lot, and she turned and looked him straight in the eyes. "Even you don't believe that."

He glanced away.

"Besides, why *pretend* to like the devil just to sell records? How do you think that affects your fans?"

"Look, Rebecca—" Mike's voice was cool and even—"I used to think you cared about me. Now I'm not so sure. I don't know what the deal is, but—"

"Mike—"

He cut her off with an angry shake of his head. "Hey, you don't want to go out with me, fine. That's your business. But I'll live my life my way. I don't need you to preach at me."

The words stung Becka's ears. She'd tried everything she had known, and nothing had worked. She was sad and frustrated and mad. OK, fine. If he didn't want to listen, if he didn't want her help, that was his business. She reached for the door, opened it, and stepped out. "If that's the way you want it, Mike, then that's the way you'll have it."

She shut the door hard and headed for the hotel. She could feel his eyes on her. A moment later she heard the limo squeal off and head down the road.

～

When Rebecca got back to the room, she snapped on the computer. A message was waiting for her.

"Mom," she asked, "has Scotty seen this?"

Mom shook her head. "I don't think so, dear. He's been in the shower for quite a while."

Rebecca nodded and clicked on the E-mail. It was a message from Z.

Rebecca: Don't throw the baby out with the bathwater. Contact me as soon as possible. Z

Rebecca frowned. "What does that mean?"

"What does what mean, honey?" Mom asked from across the room.

"'Don't throw the baby out with the bathwater.'"

Mom laughed. "Oh, that's an old expression. Your father used to use it all the time. It means don't lose sight of the big picture."

Becka scowled. "What does *that* mean?"

Mom smiled. "It means sometimes people get so caught up with a little problem that they lose sight of the overall good. You know, like not seeing the forest for the trees."

Rebecca felt more confused than ever. "I sort of understood you until you got to the trees part. I think I'll just wait to see what Z says."

Mom nodded. "Sounds like a good idea."

"I have to talk to him anyway," Rebecca continued. "I've gotten nowhere with Mike.

The big TV concert is tonight, we go home tomorrow, and not a thing has changed."

"What do you mean?"

"It's obvious Mike should quit the band. I mean, Doland is so far gone he's practically growing horns. But Mike just won't see it. I'm afraid we've wasted Z's money and our time. So we might as well—"

She came to a stop as Scott emerged from the bathroom. First there was the towel on his head, which, frankly, looked kind of stupid. Then, after he took the towel off, there was the shock of red hair sticking straight up from his forehead. Not red like a redhead— red like a fire engine.

"Scotty!" Mom half gasped, half shrieked. "Did you dye your hair?"

"Uh . . . yeah."

"Why?"

"I figured it would look cool." Scott tried to say it with a straight face, but Rebecca could tell he was pretty mortified himself.

She did her best not to snicker, but it was a losing battle.

"What?" Scott snapped. "What's wrong with it?"

"Nothing's wrong with it," Rebecca said, trying to hide her laugh with a cough. "If you're a rooster."

Anger struggled with humor on Scott's

face. Humor won out when he caught his reflection in a mirror. "I guess not everybody looks good in red," he giggled.

"You march right back into the bathroom and wash that stuff out," Mom ordered. Suddenly she looked a little scared. "It does wash out, doesn't it?"

"It's just Kool-Aid, Mom," he said. "Most of it will come out in one wash . . . unless you're a blond."

"Then go wash that Kool-Aid out of your hair this instant."

Scott turned and headed back into the bathroom. That was one experiment that had obviously failed.

Rebecca said nothing more about Scott's hair until after he'd washed it and sat drying it vigorously with a towel. "You wanted to look like a rocker, didn't you?"

Scott stopped rubbing for a minute. "I wanted to look . . . different. Like somebody else besides plain old Scott."

Rebecca nodded. "I kind of went through that a few years ago."

Scott laughed. "You mean when you got that French haircut."

"Yeah," Rebecca said, joining in the chuckle. "It did look pretty weird, didn't it?"

Scott shrugged. "Yeah." After another

moment, he continued. "So . . . you and Mike are quits?"

"We're friends. That's the way it should be, don't you think?"

"Yeah." Scott nodded. "I mean, you can't forget about Ryan. He's a great guy. But it was kind of cool to think I had a sister dating a rock star."

Rebecca smiled in spite of herself. But then she grew serious. "Scott, I'm worried. I think the band could destroy Mike . . . and by the way, I'm not sure it's doing wonders for you."

Scott shook his head. "You're way off base about the band, Beck. I know Doland's a little weird, but Jackie and Grant, they're OK. And Mike is a great guy."

Becka decided not to mince words. "Scott, . . . Doland worships the devil. He's a satanist."

"No way." Scotty almost sounded hurt. "That's just an act. It's just so they can sell records."

Rebecca shook her head. "It may have started out as an act, but it isn't anymore. And even if it is . . . think about it. They're saying that they would pretend to like the devil just to sell more records. That's kind of like selling a bunch of kids down the river for money, isn't it?"

Scott looked at her, then shrugged, as if to

say that that was just her opinion. But Rebecca could tell by the way he clammed up that he was thinking things over.

"Scott!" Mom shouted the instant he stopped drying his hair and let the towel fall around his neck. "Your hair . . . it's . . . it's yellow."

Becka put her hand to her mouth in surprise, but a laugh still escaped. "I'd say it's kind of green, too."

Scott groaned. "Oh no." Apparently the Kool-Aid wasn't as easy to wash out as he had thought.

Mom sprang into action. "Get your shirt on. We're going to the beauty parlor in the lobby to ask their advice."

"Mom . . . ," Scott complained. "The beauty parlor's for girls!"

"Sorry, Scott," Mom said as she handed him the shirt. "We've got no other choice."

With another loud groan, Scott slipped on his shirt, resigned to his fate.

As soon as they had gone out the door, Rebecca noticed the little *Z* blinking on Scott's computer. Maybe Z was calling her back. She crossed to the keyboard quickly.

9

*S*itting at the computer, Rebecca carefully explained to Z what had happened with Mike. She then asked him if he would clarify his last message about the baby and the bathwater.

Many Christians think members of a band like The Scream are not worth loving.

Rebecca quickly typed:

The guys in the band aren't bad. They're just confused. And Mike is a great guy.

Z's response came swiftly:

So why are you throwing him out with the bathwater?

Rebecca wasn't crazy about the accusation and quickly shot back:

I told him to quit the band. It's not my fault if he doesn't listen. Besides, he wanted me as a girlfriend. What about Ryan?

Z's response was simple and to the point:

Are you angry at Mike or at yourself?

Rebecca thought for a moment and then typed:

I shouldn't have let myself be attracted to him.

Z's next words gave Rebecca a sense of relief.

Wisdom is often gained at a price. You have learned. Forgive yourself and move on. Just

because Mike is not the person who should be
your boyfriend doesn't mean he can't be a boy
who is also a friend.

Rebecca nodded, then told Z about her
growing fears for Scott.
He replied:

You and Scott are doing what most Christians do
when confronted with a culture alien to them.
They either want nothing to do with its people (as
is your case) or they get so involved that they get
caught up in it (as is Scotty's).

Rebecca typed:

What do I do about Scotty?

Z replied:

Scotty's clothes and hair are not the problem. The
question is, Is he compromising his beliefs?

Rebecca quickly typed:

How will I know?

Z answered:

Start by asking him. This evening will be your last

chance to reach Mike. Be careful of Doland. And remember: "Put on all of God's armor so that you will be able to stand firm against all strategies and tricks of the Devil."

Z

Rebecca signed off, but her mind was in a whirl. What could she do to help Mike? She'd already told him he should quit the band. What else could she say? She understood why it was hard for him to leave, but the more she recognized the growing evil, the more the pluses of leaving outweighed those of staying, no matter how popular the band was.

And then she heard it. A noise. Like . . . some kind of scratching. It was coming from Mom's bedroom. She got up, went into the room, and turned on the light.

Nothing.

The sound was probably coming from the next room. Even in the best hotels you could sometimes hear people laughing or making noise in the next room. But this was more of a rubbing and scratching sound.

And then it stopped.

Rebecca waited half a minute before she shut off the light, turned, and walked back into the main room.

She flopped onto the sofa, stared out the sliding-glass door at the palm trees, and let

her mind drift back to Mike. Maybe he
didn't need to hear how he should give up
the band or stop playing his music. Instead
of hearing what he shouldn't do, maybe he
just needed to be reminded of God's great
love for him. Just because he was raised as a
pastor's son didn't mean he understood
God's love. Pastors were often overworked
and overused by their congregations. Sometimes they were so busy meeting other
people's needs that their families ended up
paying the price. It would have been easy for
Mike not to get all the attention he thought
he needed. Maybe Mike had just forgotten
how loved he was.

Scratch . . . scratch . . . scratch.

There it was again. The sound *was* coming
from Mom's room. Once again Rebecca
headed into the bedroom and switched on
the light. Once again the sound stopped.
This is ridiculous, Rebecca thought. But, ridiculous or not, the sound was driving her nuts.
And making her a little afraid, too.

She decided to play a trick of her own.
Once again she shut off the light and walked
out of the room. Only this time she tiptoed
back in without turning on the light.

Scratch . . . scratch . . . scratch. Sure enough,
the sound started again. *Scratch . . . scratch
. . . scratch.* She listened closely; then to her

surprise she realized where the sound was coming from. It came from the door that connected their room to someone else's!

Scratch . . . scratch . . . scratch. Someone in the next room was trying to open her door! The scratching sound was coming from the lock.

Someone was trying to pick the lock!

Heart pounding, Rebecca began tiptoeing out of the room. She planned to get out and race down to the lobby to tell the manager. But she wasn't even out of the room when she heard the lock click open. She turned to see the doorknob turning. Someone was coming inside.

She looked around, then quickly ducked into the closet and hid behind Mom's clothes. There were only a few dresses, a couple of blouses, a pair of pants, and a coat. Becka wished Mom had packed a bit more so she could hide herself better, but she used what she had.

Slowly she peered out through the crack of the door. In the dim light she saw two men. One was thin and scraggly looking, with a mean face. The other was big and burly and bald, with a small black beard. They quickly moved through the bedroom toward the living room. As they passed the closet, Rebecca could see that the burly man carried a large potato sack and the scraggly guy had some rope.

A cold wave of fear washed over her as she realized they were coming for her. They were planning to kidnap her.

Jesus, help me! she prayed silently.

"She ain't here," the scraggly guy called.

"Must have snuck out," the other grunted. "You think she heard us?"

"Maybe. We'd better get out of here in case she ran to get help."

"Let's go," the big man agreed. "We'll come back for her tonight when they're all asleep."

Rebecca heard the men go back through the connecting door and relock it. She waited for what felt like hours but could only have been minutes, praying and trying to calm herself. Finally, she opened the closet door and stepped out.

Light glared into her face, and a deep voice shouted, "Get her!"

Rebecca tried to run, but big meaty hands grabbed her. Another pair of hands slapped a large piece of tape over her mouth.

"Get that bag over her!" the deep voice commanded.

Rebecca felt the coarse potato sack burn her face as it was slipped over her head. Then she felt ropes tying her hands, her feet, and wrapping around the bag, binding her fast.

"Got her," the second voice said. "Doland said to take her to the warehouse."

"Right," the deep voice agreed. "We'll fry her there the same time Doland fries that drummer onstage."

Please help me, Jesus! Rebecca prayed silently and frantically.

The rough hands grabbed her, trying to pick her up. She kicked and wriggled, but she could only move in short hops. The big man quickly hoisted her up onto his shoulder.

Please, Jesus, please!

Just then, she heard the hall door open and Scott's voice. "Wait'll you see this, Beck."

She wanted to shout, but her mouth was sealed tight. She felt herself being carried toward the connecting door.

"Beck, where are you?"

Suddenly the light came on in the bedroom. She heard Scott shout and the big man's voice yelling, *"Run!"*

The next thing she knew she was dropped like, well, like a sack of potatoes, and she heard the pounding of footsteps. Moments later a very frightened Scott was pulling the bag from her face.

"You all right?"

Rebecca nodded as Scott carefully removed the tape from her mouth. "We've got to call the cops," he exclaimed.

When the tape was gone, she gasped for air. "We've got . . . we've got to warn Mike. I heard them say Doland is planning on killing him."

"What? No way!"

Becka nodded, but even now she could tell Scotty wasn't entirely buying it. He untied her, and she tried to call Mike, but there was no answer from his room.

"Wait," Scott said, looking at his watch. "He wouldn't be there now. He's at the pre-show party."

"Do you know where it is? I've got to talk to him."

"Yeah. Jackie gave me the address . . . but . . . we'll have to take a cab, and Mom's downstairs having her hair done."

"There's no time," Rebecca snapped. "Leave her a note. We've got to go!"

~

Mike stood staring at the other band members, trying to block out the sound of the party all around them.

"What about 'Army of the Night'?" Jackie Vee said. "Are we doing the rap part or not?"

"We've got to do the rap part," Doland

insisted. "When Mike goes into that soft drum beat and I start talking . . . that really gets the kids worked up."

"It gets them worked up all right," Mike replied. "We almost had a riot on our hands in Houston."

"A riot? Come on," Doland mocked. "A couple of chairs got thrown around and you call it a riot."

"Kids got hurt. *Fans* got hurt," Mike replied. *"Our* fans."

Doland threw up his hands in despair. "Nobody got hurt bad—"

"Seventeen stitches for that one girl in her forehead. I'd call that bad enough."

Doland fidgeted, barely able to contain his anger. "Oh, you're such a defender of the people now, aren't you, Mikey? Next thing you know, you'll be running for office."

Mike shook his head in disgust. He'd had it. "I'm outta here." He got up, started to leave, and then turned back. "I just want to know one thing, Doland."

"What's that?"

"If there is *anyone* or *anything* left in this world that you care about . . . besides yourself."

With that Mike turned and walked away. But Doland was already smiling that sick smile of his. Once the door shut behind

Mike, he turned to the others and grinned. "Now the party really begins."

~

It was a good fifteen minutes before Scott and Rebecca's cab pulled up.

"Twenty-two dollars?" Rebecca gulped.

The cabdriver nodded. "This is L.A., miss. There ain't no place easy to get to."

Rebecca nodded but didn't completely understand. "Here . . . I'm sorry, I've only got fifty cents left for a tip."

The cabdriver smiled. "Well, ain't this *my* lucky day."

They headed up the walk and rang the bell. Billy Phelps opened the door. "Hey, dudes. C'mon in."

"Do you know where Mike is?" Rebecca asked.

Billy scratched his head. "He just left. He and Doland had another go-around, so he took off. Doland and the guys left right after that."

"Oh no!" Rebecca said. "I've got to see him."

Billy shrugged. "Try the hotel, I guess."

"I . . . I don't have enough money for a cab."

"Don't worry about it," Billy said. "The other limo is parked in back. Just tell the driver I said it was OK. He'll take you and then come back here."

Rebecca smiled. "Thanks, Billy. Let's go, Scott."

Scott hesitated. "I'd kind of like to stay here, if it's OK, Beck."

She turned to him, not believing her ears. "After all that happened—you want to stay here?"

Scotty glanced around and lowered his voice so even Billy couldn't hear. "You don't know for certain that those guys were connected with the band."

"I heard them use Doland's name!"

"You *thought* you heard them use his name. You said yourself, you were inside that gunnysack, getting thrown all around."

"Scotty . . ."

"He can ride with us to the gig," Billy said, trying to be helpful. "That way he can help us check everything out."

"C'mon, Beck," Scott pleaded. "My last chance to ride with the biggest band in the country . . . to a nationally televised concert. . . ."

Rebecca wasn't sure what to do. But she knew she had to get to the hotel as fast as she could. "You say Doland's already left?"

Billy nodded.

That gave her some comfort.

"Don't worry, big sister," Billy said with a grin. "I'll take care of little brother here."

Rebecca slowly nodded. "OK . . . but be careful." With that she headed off for the limo.

~

As soon as Rebecca was out of sight, Billy turned to Scott. "So, you want a beer?"

"Uh . . . yeah, sure." Guilt washed over him the minute the words were out of his mouth, but he just clenched his teeth. So what if he was underage? So what if he hated the taste of beer? What he hated even worse was looking like he didn't fit in. Besides, one little beer couldn't hurt, could it?

A few seconds later, Billy had shoved a brew into his hand and headed off, leaving Scott to wander the party, pretending to sip his beer and trying not to look like a geek. He failed in both departments.

It didn't take long to notice that the people here were even stranger than the ones who'd been at the backstage party. Nearly all of them were dressed in black, and several had symbols painted on their faces. As Scott walked around, he realized there were also lots of drugs being passed around.

Scott managed to avoid the occasional

joint that was passed through the crowd, but it became clearer by the second that staying had been a mistake. Seeing the plastic skulls, daggers, and pentagrams all over the place didn't help matters either.

He tried convincing himself to be more open-minded, to pretend they were just decorations—like a perpetual Halloween party. That might have worked, too, if he hadn't spotted people in the corner chanting some kind of gobbledygook and others in the kitchen burning black candles and joining hands in a séance.

So much for open-mindedness.

Scott began looking for Billy to get a ride home. He found him making out with some girl in another room. He looked pretty busy, but Scott had to ask him anyway. "Hey, Billy . . ."

"Not now, sport," Billy said without looking up. "Come back later."

Scott backed out of the room, unsure how he was going to get out of there. He decided to see if the limo had returned. But as soon as he stepped into the backyard, he sensed something wrong. His head began to hurt slightly, the way it had in past demonic encounters. He spotted Jackie and Grant standing with about a dozen others near a small bonfire and headed toward them.

As he approached, he nearly ran into Doland, who was walking up the driveway carrying a small cat. The rocker turned and glared at him wildly but said nothing. Instead, he continued past him and walked to the center of the small circle of people.

Scotty watched, swallowing back his fear as Doland raised the squirming cat over his head and toward the fire. The poor animal was in a panic, wriggling and writhing, desperately trying to get away.

"So, almighty one," Doland called out, "give to us portions of your power as we offer this sacrifice to you."

Sacrifice! Doland was about to sacrifice that poor cat to the devil. Before he could think about it, Scotty shouted, "Stop it! What do you think you're doing?"

The group turned and stared at him. But it was Doland's gaze that frightened him the most. In the glow of the fire, the singer's eyes seemed to shine. He looked like a wild man as his body began to shake . . . like someone losing control of his will . . . like someone who had just opened himself up to another spirit.

Realizing he'd used up all of his courage with that first shout, Scott began to pray under his breath. "Dear Jesus, please help me. Please step in here with your power."

Doland shook more violently.

But the shaking was different. Scott's prayer was having an effect on the man. Scott bore down and prayed harder until, suddenly, Doland stopped shaking and took a step toward him.

"You want this cat, punk?" Doland yelled, still holding the wiggling animal above his head.

Scott nodded. He wanted to speak but didn't trust his voice.

Doland's smile twisted across his face . . . and he hurled the cat directly at Scotty. He managed to get his hands up to prevent his face from being scratched, but his arms weren't so lucky. The cat's claws tore into him, drawing blood from three deep cuts.

Scott yelped in pain. Even so, he was glad to see the cat land safely on the lawn and bolt into the night. Slowly now, he backed away from the others. Doland continued glaring at him but didn't come after him.

"That's right!" Doland shouted. "Better get out of here, you little puke. . . . Get out while you still can."

N

Rebecca's limo pulled into the big, circular driveway in front of the hotel. She looked up just in time to see Mike getting into a taxi-

cab that started to pull away. She leaped
from the limo and chased the cab down the
drive, shouting and waving her hands.
"Stop! Wait a minute! Mike! Stop!"

But Mike never saw her, and the cab never
stopped.

Frustrated, she turned around only to see
the limo start to pull away as well. Again she
ran, shouting and waving. This time she was
heard. The limo stopped, and the driver
rolled down the window. He was a kindly
looking, gray-haired gentleman. "Yes, miss?"

Rebecca was still catching her breath.
"Can . . . can you take me to the auditorium?"

The limo driver looked at his watch. "I suppose so, miss. But we'll have to leave right
this moment so I'll have enough time to
swing back and pick up the others from the
party."

Rebecca looked back toward the hotel.
She really should see Mom, but there just
wasn't time.

She reached for the back door, climbed
in, and they were off. The minutes dragged
by as the limo fought the crosstown traffic,
but at last they arrived in front of the auditorium. She jumped out and headed for the
doors.

᠕

Scott held firmly to Billy Phelps's jacket as they pulled up on the motorcycle.

"Thanks for the ride, Billy," Scott shouted as he climbed off the bike.

Billy nodded. "No problem, man. Listen, I've gotta go in and check some wires. . . . Here's the money you earned working with the crew. I really don't think it'd be a good idea for Doland to see you after what happened at the party. So you just stay out front, OK?"

Scott nodded and took the money; then his eyes widened. "Wow! A hundred bucks. I didn't work enough hours for that."

"Don't worry. . . . Consider it hazard pay for those cat scratches," he chuckled. "Besides, the other guys on the crew drink up that much just in beer. See you around, Scott."

"See ya, Billy."

᠕

The lights were off. The room was illuminated only by the flickering flame of the black candle in the center of the kitchen table. Tommy Doland, the large bald man, and three groupies sat there. The chant began, low at first, but then gradually increasing until it became a shout: "All must die! All must die! All must die!"

And with each word, Tommy felt the power within him growing stronger. Tonight would be the night.

10

*R*ebecca was one
of fifty teenagers inside the auditorium
crowding to get through the backstage door.
A huge man with a green beard and a red-
dot tattoo in the center of his forehead
stood blocking the entrance. As far as
Rebecca could tell, he only spoke four
words: "Not on the list." That's what he'd

said to the girl in front of her, just as he had said it to a dozen others before that.

Rebecca had had no problem getting inside the auditorium, but she'd been waiting a long time here, working her way to that burly guard as one teen after another tried to persuade him to let him or her pass. Each time, he scanned a tiny piece of paper in his hands and said, "Not on the list." There must not have been very many names on the list, Rebecca thought, since the piece of paper was no larger than a bubble-gum wrapper. Finally, it was her turn.

"Hi," she said. "Remember me? I was here the other night."

The big man showed no sign of recognition.

"I'm Rebecca Williams. I'm a friend of Mike Parsek's."

"Not on the list," the guard said, barely glancing at the paper.

"No," Rebecca said. "I'm on the list. I'm sure of it. You didn't look close enough. Rebecca Williams."

The guard looked again. "Not on the list."

Rebecca shook her head, fighting the panic that threatened to wash over her. "No! That can't be right. It's very important that I see Mike before the show. His life may be in danger. Maybe it's under Becka Williams.

Look up that name; he calls me that sometimes."

The guard's eyes glazed over. Rebecca felt
the girl behind her press against her. "Hurry
up, will you?" she muttered.

Rebecca turned around. "No, this is not
what you think. I *am* a friend of Mike's, and
he said—"

The girl made a face. "He dumped you."

Rebecca was shocked. "He did not . . . no
one dumped anyone. We were just friends
and . . . if anyone dumped anyone, it was I
who did the dumping. . . ."

Again Rebecca turned back and looked at
the guard, hoping somehow he would
remember her.

"Not on the list" was all he said.

Mike Parsek stood behind the curtain. The
auditorium looked the same as it had for the
previous show, except the lighting was more
elaborate and there was one new piece of
equipment—an even larger fire cannon. As
Mike strode onto the stage, Billy Phelps
came out from behind the control board.

"So what do you think of her, Mike?" Billy
asked, looking at the cannon.

"It's a monster."

"You should see it fire. I tested it earlier

today, and the fireball went about forty feet up into the rafters. I thought it was going to blast right through the roof."

Mike frowned. "What about the crowd? Are we going to be raining fire on them?"

Billy shook his head. "No, it dissipates into nothing after that initial blast. But I'd sure hate to be in that first forty feet. There'd be nothing left but cinders and ash."

Mike nodded, looking slowly along the length of the huge shiny black barrel until he came to the opening at the end. "You're sure this thing is safe?"

"Sure," Phelps said. "It's got a warranty and everything. We're going to fire it off about three times during your solo at half strength and then at full strength at the end like we usually do."

Mike stared into the large black hole at the end of the barrel—and a very strange and uneasy feeling swept over him.

He shook it off, frustrated. He'd been listening to Rebecca Williams too much.

By showtime Rebecca had tried the other five backstage entrances with the same results. In fact, she was pretty sure the guards must be related because they all looked alike and said the same thing. Except for the last guy. Instead of "Not on the list," he chose to say "Beat it, bimbo" to every girl and "Beat it, jerk-boy" to every guy.

Finally, the lights dimmed and the music began. Rebecca realized there was nothing more to do and decided to find her seat and watch the show.

The crowd was even larger and rowdier than before. For good reason. There were TV cameras everywhere. It was a big event, all right, and the band rose to the occasion. During the first song, as Rebecca made her way to her seat, Tommy Doland was already cutting loose. He was frantic, a madman with a microphone. And the crowd hung on his every word.

"Over here! Becka, over here!"

She turned toward the familiar voice and saw Scott waving at her, pointing to the empty seat. "We're over here!" he shouted.

She moved through the crowd toward him, yelling, "I thought you were backstage!"

Scott shrugged as she finally arrived. "Doland showed up at the party and some weird stuff started happening. I'm kind of fired. But Billy gave me a ride over and paid me a hundred bucks!"

Becka looked at him, caught by one part of what he'd said. "What kind of weird stuff?"

Over the pounding music Scott explained

the intended animal sacrifice and showed
her the scratches. "They don't hurt too
bad," he shouted. "Billy poured hydrogen
peroxide on them before we took off."

Rebecca's stomach was churning again.
Something was going to happen. She was cer-
tain of it. "I never got to Mike," she yelled.
"Security wouldn't let me pass."

By now the concert was in full swing. TV
cameras rolled, and The Scream gave the
performance of a lifetime. Doland never let
up. His frenetic energy was more than
human. But the others did their part as well.
Jackie Vee's fingers flew over the strings of
his guitar as though he were carving an intri-
cate sculpture out of a wall of sound. But it
was the rhythm section that really domi-
nated. Mike Parsek was at his peak, pounding and driving out the beat as Grant
Simone tracked him lick for lick on the bass.

They were phenomenal, and everyone in
the auditorium knew it.

It wasn't until Mike launched into his solo
that Rebecca noticed the new fire cannon. It
was huge, but that wasn't what stopped her.
There was something oddly familiar about it.
Then a chill washed over her. . . . It was the
cannon from her dream.

As Mike increased the pace of his solo,
Rebecca's heart pounded. She had to warn

him. Suddenly, a terrible blast shot a huge tongue of fire into the air above the crowd. Everyone screamed, including Rebecca.

"Take it easy," Scott shouted to her. "It's all part of the show."

Becka's eyes shot to him. "Not this time, Scotty! This time I think Doland is—"

The sentence was cut off by another mighty blast, even bigger than the last. The crowd screamed as never before, and Mike picked up the pace.

Rebecca caught sight of Doland as he cheered Mike on from the edge of the stage. Like at the previous shows, one by one the other members of the band left the stage, leaving Mike to carry the show with a fury of drum rhythms.

Only this time, Doland was moving away from the stage and going behind the curtain. *What's he up to?* Rebecca thought. A moment later she caught a glimpse of him by the control panel . . . all by himself. Billy Phelps had moved away from the panel to watch Mike along with everyone else.

"Scott, let me borrow those binoculars!" Rebecca shouted. He handed them to her, and she focused in on Doland. He was adjusting something, turning a knob.

Just like my dream! she thought. Only

instead of a gnarled and twisted claw touching the control panel, it was Doland.

Rebecca began to pray. But when she looked up at the barrel of the cannon, she groaned. It was changing direction, slowly turning toward Mike . . . just as it had in her dream.

Rebecca bolted, pushing her way through the crowd. She knew she'd never get close enough to warn Mike, but she had to try. *Jesus, Jesus, help me!*

Scotty must have realized something was up—he'd moved in behind her. But it was wall-to-wall people, and no one was moving.

"Excuse me! Excuse me, please!" Rebecca shouted over and over again, but no one listened.

"Out of the way!" Scott suddenly yelped. "This girl's sick. She's going to puke any second! Let us through!"

The crowd instantly parted, and Becka and Scott squeezed toward the stage.

Mike was nearing the peak of his solo. He was concentrating on his playing so intently that he didn't even notice the cannon barrel turning toward him. In just a few seconds, it would be pointing directly at him!

"Mike!" Rebecca shouted. "The cannon! The cannon!"

Scott joined in. "The cannon, Mike! Get out of there!"

But it was no use. They could not be heard.

Rebecca continued pushing through the crowd. The cannon was aimed directly at Mike as he launched into the highlight of his solo. In just a few moments, it would fire.

"Please, Lord!" Rebecca prayed out loud now, not caring who heard her. "Save him. Somehow, save him!"

The drums drove and pounded like never before. Rebecca was so close she could feel the vibrations coming from the cannon as it prepared to ignite.

There were only seconds left. She shoved and pushed harder, but they were still too far from the stage. They weren't going to make it. She wouldn't be able to warn him.

She felt Scott grab her. "Get on my back," he shouted. "Hurry."

Rebecca climbed on a seat and then on top of Scott's shoulders. She began waving frantically. "Mike! Mike!"

The cannon began to shake.

"MIKE! MIKE!"

And then, suddenly, he looked up and saw her waving.

She pointed frantically toward the cannon.

He turned and saw it pointed directly at him.

And then it happened. There was a colossal explosion as the cannon fired. Becka screamed, but Mike was already in the air. He was leaping off his drum riser, flying through the flames as they ignited his platform, his drums, everything around him.

The crowd screamed as the nearby curtains caught fire. Panic and chaos filled the auditorium. People cried and yelled and stampeded.

Becka managed to catch a final glimpse of Mike before she tumbled from Scott's shoulders. He was staggering to his feet. He was unhurt. He looked a little worn and bruised, but he was unhurt.

"Thank you, dear God," Rebecca prayed as she was jostled this way and that. "Thank you. . . ."

∾

In all the confusion that followed, Rebecca and Scott managed to slip by the guard at the backstage door. Once past him, they hurried down the long corridor that ran underneath the stage. When they came out the other side, they saw Mike helping Billy, Jackie, and Grant clear the instruments and sound equipment away from the charred and smoldering curtain.

"Mike!" Rebecca shouted as she ran to him. He opened his arms, and they embraced for a long moment before she finally pulled back. "I've been trying to warn you for hours." Her voice was choked with tears. "Thank God you're all right." She hugged him again, then continued, "Someone tried to kidnap me at the hotel, and I heard them mention Doland's name and something about frying the drummer onstage and, and—" she felt her eyes burn as the tears cascaded down her cheeks— "I tried so hard to warn you."

"You *did* warn me," Mike said softly. He held her back and looked deeply into her eyes. "You saved my life."

Again she embraced him, so happy that he was alive.

"Too bad."

The voice made her grow cold. She turned around to see Doland sneering. "You spoiled the show." He stalked toward them menacingly. "I wanted to burn you right onstage, Mikey. It would've been the best publicity stunt ever. Now I just get to fire you the normal way."

"You can't fire me," Mike said, his voice trembling slightly.

"And why is that?"

"Because I quit. You're one sick puppy, Doland, and I want nothing to do with you or your music."

"Oh, I'm crushed," Doland sneered. "Lucky for me drummers are a dime a dozen. We can find another one anytime we want."

"Not with me, you won't."

Becka turned to see Jackie Vee stepping forward.

"Or me," Grant Simone said, moving up beside him. "I'm quitting too. We're all quitting."

Jackie Vee nodded. "You've gone too far this time, Doland."

For a second Doland seemed lost, but only for a second. He spun back around to Rebecca and Scott. His features began to contort, and his voice started to emit a strange, growling sound.

Rebecca braced herself. She knew what was coming next.

The hideous growl formed into deep guttural words:

"This is your fault," the voice growled. **"You are the ones who must pay."**

The other band members stepped back in alarm as Doland's face contorted until it was

unrecognizable. Becka stood still, watching.
This was the hatred she had seen, had felt
from the moment she'd first stepped off the
shuttle bus and Doland had turned to stare
at her. Only now its fury was full, boring into
her with amazing intensity. For an instant
she saw a grotesque gargoyle mask forming
over Doland's face. She knew exactly what it
was. She'd seen it in other encounters.

She forced herself to blink and clear her
vision. Now it was gone. Only Doland remained.

But she wasn't fooled. She knew the battle
was finally in the open.

He started toward her, and she opened
her mouth to speak, to pray, but nothing
came out. Alarm washed over her. She
couldn't speak! It wasn't fear, she knew that.
But she didn't know what it was.

Could this be a new power she had never
encountered before? *Father, help me,* she
cried out silently. And as she did so, peace
washed over her.

But still she couldn't speak. Then she heard
Scotty praying softly behind her. "Deliver us
from evil, O Lord. Deliver us from evil."

Doland hesitated, shooting Scott an angry
glare. And then he continued toward her,
toward them. He was four feet away now,
sneering, closing in.

And still Rebecca was held in silence.

Then, miraculously, another voice joined Scott's prayer. It was Mike Parsek. He spoke, barely above a whisper, but he was definitely praying. "Deliver us from evil, O Lord. Deliver us from evil."

At that moment it was as though a gag were removed, and Rebecca's voice was released. Swift understanding came to her: God had been giving Mike the opportunity to step out in faith. And he'd done so! Now she was allowed to move in and help him out. She took a slow deep breath and spoke clearly: "In the name of the Lord Jesus Christ, I command you to stop."

Instantly, Doland stopped moving toward her.

Becka swallowed, then continued, "I speak to the demonic force controlling Tommy Doland and to the demon within him." Her voice was stronger now. "In the name of Jesus Christ and by the power of his blood, I command you to leave. Come out from Doland. Now! Come out and be gone."

For an instant the gargoyle-like creature reappeared, as if leaving Doland. But then, suddenly, it grinned and settled back inside of him.

"What's going on?" Mike whispered.

Now it was Doland grinning. He took another step toward Becka.

"I said come out of him," Rebecca ordered. "In the name of Jesus Christ."

Again the form appeared to be coming out; again it settled back inside of Doland.

"He doesn't want it to go," Scott explained.

Rebecca continued to hold Doland's glare. Despite his hatred and the hideous sneer, she felt sorry for him. Very, very sorry.

Mike looked on, then quietly spoke. "He's condemned himself."

Slowly, sadly, Becka nodded. But there was more work to be done. Her voice broke through the silence, bold and confident. "In the name of Jesus, I command you to leave. Leave and do no more harm to these people."

Instantly, Doland staggered back. It was as if he was suddenly afraid to even look at them. He retreated another step or two before turning and slinking across the stage.

"Remember," Becka called, "you are bound from ever harming these people again. We command that in the power and authority of Jesus Christ."

All watched in silence as Tommy Doland exited the stage.

A couple of crew members started to mumble. They'd obviously seen nothing like this before. And, as the encounter faded, Becka felt the weakness return to her body. It was one thing to speak in faith, to feel the power of the Holy Spirit surging through her, but it was quite another to be plain ol' Rebecca Williams.

~

The following day Mike agreed to take Rebecca, Scott, and Mom to the airport. The four of them had spent most of the night together, and by the end of the evening Mike had not only quit the band but had recommitted his life to Jesus Christ. And, thanks to Mom's gentle urgings, he had even agreed to visit his parents.

"No promises," he said, "but I'll give it another shot."

Now, as they stood at the gate, ready to board the plane, Mike turned to Becka one last time. "And if it's OK with you, I really do want to be your friend."

She looked up at him, swallowing back the tightness growing in her throat.

He continued, "You're one of the few people I know who cares about me because I'm me . . . and not just because I was a member of some big-shot band."

She nodded and looked at the ground. It was important that he not see her tears. Saying good-bye was harder than she had expected.

"Oh, and, Scott—" he turned toward her

little brother—"I've got something for you."
He reached down into a small bag and
pulled out a Scream T-shirt. "I'm afraid it
got a little singed in the fire, but I think
you'll like the way it turned out."

He held it up. The shirt was perfectly fine
. . . except that one letter was scorched.
Where it had once read "Army of the
Night," part of the *N* was burned and
smudged so it now read "Army of the Light."

Scott beamed as he took it. "Army of the
Light. Now *that's* cool."

A minute later they said their final good-
byes, and Becka, Scott, and Mom walked
down the ramp toward their plane. Rebecca
could feel Mike still standing there, still watching. And she could feel her eyes once again
starting to burn with moisture. But they
weren't tears of sadness. They were tears of
gratitude. She was grateful they had decided
to simply stay friends. But she was even more
grateful that once again, Mike Parsek had
found, and was getting acquainted with, his
very best Friend.

On the plane Rebecca couldn't help but
notice that Scott was looking more like his
old self. "Hey, Scotty, where are the torn

jeans?" she teased. "You look halfway normal."

Scott shrugged. "I don't know. I guess I kind of lost interest in all that stuff. I mean, I used to think it was, like, really being real . . . but there was an awful lot about those people that wasn't real at all. All that fake booze and fashion and stuff just to psych out the audience . . ."

Mom nodded. "It's kind of strange how things turned out. I mean, at first The Scream and all of their fans were people I'd want to avoid like the plague. But if we had, then Mike might not have returned to his faith."

Scott agreed. "God really does care . . . about everybody. I guess we can't write anybody off."

"But that doesn't mean we have to be like them," Rebecca said, giving him a teasing smile.

"Yeah," Scott sighed as he rubbed his hair, which still had a touch of yellow and green in it. "I wonder what the guys on my baseball team are going to say about this."

In just a few hours the family was heading down another airline ramp. Only this time it was at home. Becka was the first to see Ryan. His jet black hair and sparkling smile made him stand out from the crowd. In one hand he clutched an envelope, in the other a welcome-home bouquet of flowers.

Before she knew it, she found herself running down the last few steps of the ramp to greet him. As they embraced, she held him tighter than she had ever held him before. She'd had no idea how much she had missed him. And when they separated, she was surprised at the fresh tears springing to her eyes.

"Hey," he asked in concern, "are you OK?"

She nodded, unable to speak.

"Are you sure? I mean, you're crying. Why are you crying?"

She could only roll her eyes. Men . . . would they ever learn?

"Hey, Ryan," Scott called.

"Hey, Scott. Hi, Mrs. Williams."

"Flowers for me?" Scott joked. "Why, Ryan, you shouldn't have."

"You're right. I shouldn't, and I wouldn't." He faked a punch at Scotty and gave the flowers to Becka.

"Ryan . . . they're beautiful." Once again her eyes started welling up with moisture, and once again Ryan frowned.

"Maybe it's allergies," he said. "You should probably have that looked into."

Before Rebecca could answer, Scott was doing what he did best . . . butting in. "What is that?" he asked, motioning to the manila envelope in Ryan's other hand.

"Four tickets to New Mexico. They came in the mail a few days ago," Ryan said. "They're from Z."

"Z?" Becka asked.

Ryan nodded.

"Cool," Scott quipped. "Sounds like another assignment is about to begin."

Rebecca let out a low, quiet sigh. At the moment she'd had enough assignments. Right now she just wanted to go home and get some rest. She was pleased to feel Ryan take her hand as they turned and started through the airport to pick up their luggage. She had no idea what awaited them in New Mexico—or what spiritual counterfeit she'd have to face next. But for now she was just grateful to be home . . . and to feel her hand in Ryan's.

AUTHOR'S NOTE

As I continue writing this series, I have two equal and opposing concerns. First, I don't want the reader to be too frightened of the devil. Compared to Jesus Christ, Satan is a wimp. The two aren't even in the same league. Although the supernatural evil in these books is based on a certain amount of fact, it's important to understand the awesome protection Jesus Christ offers to all those who have committed their lives to him.

This brings me to my second and somewhat opposing concern: Although the powers of darkness are nothing compared to the power of Jesus Christ and the authority he has given his followers, spiritual warfare is not something we casually stroll into. The situations in these novels are extreme to create suspense and drama. But if you should find yourself involved in something even vaguely similar, don't confront it alone. Find an older, more mature Christian (such as a parent, pastor, or youth leader) to talk to. Ask that person to check out the situation to see what is happening and to help you deal with it.

Yes, we have the victory through Christ, but we should never send in inexperienced soldiers to fight the battle.

Oh, and one final note. When this series was conceived, there were really no bad guys on the Internet. Unfortunately that has changed. Today there are plenty of people out there on the Internet trying to draw young folks into dangerous situations. Although the characters in this series trust Z, if you should run into a similar situation, be smart. Anyone can *sound* kind and under-standing, but their intentions may be entirely different. All that to say, don't take candy from strangers you see . . . or trust those you don't.

Bill